# *Flickering Hope*

# Flickering Hope

Sharat Sabharwal

Rupa . Co

Published 2009 by
Rupa . Co

7/16, Ansari Road, Daryaganj,
New Delhi 110 002

*Sales Centres:*

Allahabad Bengalooru Chandigarh Chennai
Hyderabad Jaipur Kathmandu
Kolkata Mumbai



Typeset by
Mindways Design
1410 Chiranjiv Tower
43 Nehru Place
New Delhi 110 019

Printed in India by
Nutech Photolithographers
B-240, Okhla Industrial Area, Phase-I,
New Delhi 110 020, India

*To my father*
*Dr Ishwar Swarup*
*an angel, a doting father and a master story-teller*

The public address system of the ferry crackled to life, announcing the end of my journey across the English Channel for the umpteenth time: 'Mesdames et Messieurs, nous sommes arrives a Calais.'

My physician-turned-entrepreneur father had set up a pharmaceuticals factory that had, over the years, signed a number of collaboration contracts with British and French companies, thereby entailing my frequent visits to these countries. I preferred journey by train and ferry between London and Paris since travel by air was too clinical for my liking and the Channel Tunnel was yet to be opened. A journey by train and ferry, on the other hand, gave me an opportunity to sit back and relax after a hectic work schedule. The fish and chips meal with hot tea on board the ferry was an added attraction for me. This time, however, the sea had been very rough and churned my insides out. Seasickness had overpowered me soon after the ferry left Dover. I had sat slumped in my seat with eyes shut, counting each second that passed. The announcement of our impending arrival at the Calais port came as a big relief.

I suddenly realised I had not gone across to the French immigration counter on the ferry to get my passport stamped. I lumbered unsteadily across to the immigration counter . The immigration officer had wound up his papers and was peeved at my request for immigration clearance at that late stage. He muttered under his breath and then asked me in an authoritative tone why I had not presented myself earlier when repeated announcements had been made for immigration check. I apologised and said I had been too sick to react to them.

Looking at my dishevelled hair and drawn expression, the man could surely make out that I was not lying. Nonetheless, he was clearly reluctant to pull out the tools of his trade, now securely packed in his bag. At this point, two more unfortunate seasick beings landed up. One look at them and the immigration officer went 'Ooh la la!' in a tone of exasperation. At long last, better sense prevailed and the officer proceeded to pull out his stamps. The prospect of being pushed back to England had mercifully receded. My passport containing a valid visa was thoroughly examined. A series of irrelevant questions followed, no doubt the result of the officer's irritated state of mind, and were politely answered. A frequent traveller, I had had a similar brush with immigration officers elsewhere and knew that you don't lock horns with them. Their authority at the time of your entry into a country is next only to that of the Lord Almighty. Finally to my relief, the stamp of approval came down on my passport. I uttered a grudging 'Merci' and proceeded to the ferry's exit. The craft had come to a halt and stabilised. My auricular fluid too was finally showing signs of settling down.

It was half past five in the evening when I walked up to the railway platform to catch a train to Paris. It was pitch dark and the November air was chilly but refreshing after my just-concluded ordeal in that overheated wobbly ferry. I made my way to the nearest compartment, put my baggage on the luggage rack and settled down in a window seat in the middle of the compartment. There were just two other persons around. A bearded man sitting across from me, five or six rows of seats ahead. I could see only his profile and he appeared to be an Asian. And a pretty girl in a seat across the aisle who was craning her neck repeatedly, looking out for someone.

I started skimming through some business papers. The train departed in about ten minutes. Some more places behind me had been occupied. The Asian had reclined his seat and was probably asleep. The young girl had been joined by her boyfriend and the two were now locked in a passionate embrace. I discreetly turned away from them, but the tinted window glass kept flashing the image of the seat opposite. The couple's embrace had tightened and the girl was resisting the excessive advances of her lover. How familiar, I thought. Only a couple of decades ago, I had been possessed by the same passion that made me oblivious to my surroundings when it came to the woman I loved. I was not too old – still in my mid forties, but it seemed as if ages had passed since then. 'Don't indulge in voyeurism!' admonished a voice within me, but I could not resist watching the scene for a few more seconds. The couple's ardour was so refreshing, so symbolic of the constant resurgence of life. A new generation takes over where an earlier one leaves off. The cycle of life moves on inexorably. In the next few seconds, I had dozed off.

I woke up with a start as I felt the gentle pressure of a hand on my shoulder. The Asian was smiling at me, 'Aren't you Lalith?'

*Lalith* – his manner of pronouncing my name took me back those long-gone years I had spent in Paris. The Asian had to be my Sri Lankan friend from my French stint twenty years ago.

'Hey! Sunil Wickramsinghe, right?'

'Absolutely right!' he beamed, as I got up from my seat, squeezing his hand.

'You haven't changed at all,' Sunil said, making himself comfortable in the seat next to mine.

'Well, I haven't put on much weight and my hair is intact. But what's with you? Not a single black hair in the beard and no hair on the head. No wonder it took me a few seconds to place you!'

'My head, old chap, was never very fertile. You know it too well. Not much in there. And now its exterior has also become barren. Nothing grows!' Sunil guffawed as he always did after making a wisecrack.

'Where do you live now? In Paris?' I asked.

'No, old chap. Soon after you left France at the end of your apprenticeship, we moved to Sri Lanka because I could not find a job here. But we came back after some years and have been in Toulouse for almost fifteen years. That's where they need people like me. I work in an ancillary factory of the Airbus Industrie and head its production unit. For a foreigner, I haven't done too badly. What about you?'

'I manage our pharmaceuticals factory with my brother. We have expanded a great deal over the years. Lot of work. Keeps me busy and brings me to Paris quite often. How is Brigitte? Any children?'

'Brigitte is fine. Still performing the Herculean task of teaching English to the French. Our boy, the only child, is now sixteen.' Sunil paused a little and then asked, 'How big is your family?'

'I am a lone traveller, my friend,' I answered with a quiet smile. Sunil looked perplexed but did not probe further.

'I say, old chap, I had given up hope of ever seeing you again! The fault was mine. I didn't stay in touch with you after going back to Sri Lanka. We are meeting after ... let's see ... one has lost count ...' he reflected for a few seconds, 'some twenty years?'

'Right.'

'It's so nice – such a pleasant surprise – to see you again old chap.' The expression 'old chap' was as recurrent in Sunil's speech as it had been twenty years ago.

'You can't imagine how happy I too am to see you,' I told him.

Even as I uttered those words, a seed of doubt arose in my mind. Was it a feeling of happiness – pure and simple? However, I suppressed it. Sunil was after all an old friend. A kind, generous, warm person. I still remembered the first time I had met him. Having decided to embark upon production of some medicines under licence from a French company called Remedes France SA, my father had sent me to do a year's apprenticeship with their factory in the suburbs of Paris. Remedes had business interests in many countries and the chemists I worked with knew English. However, it was a good opportunity to learn French and I had enrolled for evening classes at L'Institut Catholique in the sixth district of Paris. Ours was a group of around fifteen students from different countries and Sunil was one of them. After we finished our first class, Sunil, gregarious guy that he was, introduced himself to me, 'Old chap, your name tells me you are from India. I am from Sri Lanka. Sunil Wickramsinghe.'

Feeling a little lost in Paris, I had welcomed the company of someone from a country closer home. Our friendship had grown. Sunil was a few years older than me. He had come to England when he was twenty, worked hard to get a degree in aeronautical engineering and had got married to Brigitte, a French girl who was studying English in London. They were now in Paris. Brigitte worked in a language school while Sunil was still looking out for a job. He had joined French classes to improve his employment prospects.

This was the same good friend I had come across after such a long time. But he belonged to a chapter of my life that I had long buried in some unknown corner of my mind – a chapter that I had initially lived each day of my life but later deliberately attempted to erase all memory of. And now a character from that chapter was sitting next to me in flesh and blood. Would he say anything that would open my old wounds? I hoped not. And yet he was one person who was likely to be in the know of things at this end. Each time he opened his mouth to say something; my heart would leap – would he? And each time he finished saying something, he would look expectantly at me as if wanting me to enquire about other friends. Was I wrong in assuming that those old wounds had healed completely? Was that chapter truly dead and gone? I was getting ever more perplexed.

Sunil and I chatted for some more time and then he dozed off. He got up as the train was approaching Paris.

'Old chap, I leave for Toulouse early tomorrow morning. Hope we will now remain in touch,' he said pulling out his visiting card from his pocket. An uneasy pause followed and then he added, 'Old chap, I wonder if you have been in touch with Emilie.'

'No.'

'We had heard of what had happened. You may be interested in knowing that she is in Paris. We have not been in touch with her very often, but let me give you her phone number,' Sunil said.

Before I could say anything, he took out his pocket diary, wrote down a phone number at the back of his visiting card and handed it over to me.

We collected our belongings, said goodbye and then Sunil was gone, leaving me behind with his visiting card and the unsolicited phone number at its back. I had half a mind to tear it up, but then thought otherwise as it also contained Sunil's contact particulars. I kept the card in my pocket.

The cab dropped me at Hotel des Alpes – a small establishment in a crowded street not very far from the Champs Elysees. It was a homely joint unlike big impersonal hotels, and more importantly, its tariff suited my pocket. I was a familiar figure as I had stayed there for the last ten years each time I came to Paris.

The receptionist welcomed me with a broad smile, 'Nice to see you, Monsieur Khanna.'

The check-in formalities completed, I retired to my room. It had been a long and exhausting day. I hit the bed straight away and dozed off.

I got up with a start, my body drenched in sweat. There was no sign of daylight. My watch showed it was twenty minutes past one. Emilie's memory was slowly getting hold of my mind. Should I see her? She probably had a family of her own and they might not like an intruder. And what would a meeting with her do to me? Over the years, I had built a well-ordered cocoon around myself – work, my favourite golf and voluntary work at an orphanage in my spare time. A meeting with Emilie would blow it all apart. Would I ever be able to resurrect it? The encounter with Sunil had already produced a chink in my protective shell, or perhaps the shell had never been perfect.

A neon sign flashed through the net curtains across the window. Strangely enough, the hotel staff had not rolled down the window shutter despite the extremely cold weather outside. I rolled it down to cut off light. The total darkness that ensued was unbearable.

I switched on the bedside lamp and called the reception. A sleepy voice answered, 'Allo, oui.'

'Would you have a tranquiliser?' I asked.

'No, Monsieur, we don't keep that sort of stuff in our first aid box. That would be illegal, you know. Is Monsieur all right? We could, if you wish, arrange to take you to an emergency clinic.'

'No thanks, it's nothing serious.'

The phone rang within five minutes. It was the receptionist. The night porter, he said, had picked up a strip of tranquilisers for his wife, who was taking the medicine under medical advice. The tablets were in his bag. A mild dose of Valium. Could he send one up?

'Yes, yes,' I said in an eager tone. At that moment, the small Valium tablet seemed to be my only saviour against the storm that was looming large over the patched up fabric of my life.

The night porter arrived with the medicine.

'Would you please tell the receptionist to wake me up at seven tomorrow morning?'

'Certainly, Monsieur, shall do that. Sleep well for now.'

The tablet worked and I was asleep in a few minutes.

The phone had been ringing for some time when I answered it.

'Your wake-up call, Monsieur.'

I uttered 'Merci' in a groggy tone.

Sensing that my voice during the first call was not alert enough, the receptionist put through another call within five minutes. By this time, I was wide awake, my head a little heavy. I rolled up the shutter. It was still dark outside but dawn was just breaking. My spirits rose a little. It has been my experience that after a lonely night of fear and apprehension, the arrival of a new day always brings hope, if of nothing else, at least of one's ability to cope with the tricky situation.

I had to reach the head office of Remedes France at nine. It was a few minutes to eight when I got out of the hotel. I rushed in the light drizzle to Café de Nice across the street. This was my favourite eating joint.

'Ah, who do I see? Monsieur Khanna, you haven't been here for months. We missed you.' Pierre, the proprietor was as warm as ever.

'Well, India is not next door, Pierre. I come only when work brings me,' I said, taking a seat on a tall stool across the bar counter from Pierre. Some others were already having their coffee-and-croissants breakfast.

'Will you please serve, Monsieur?' Pierre told a girl I was seeing for the first time.

'What would you like to drink?' the girl asked.

Before I could answer, Pierre intervened, 'Monsieur Khanna always takes chocolat chaud with croissants for breakfast, my little one.' Turning towards me, he explained, 'She is new here, you see.'

'Employed her recently?'

'Well, she is not an employee. Ever since my wife left, I was too lonely and now Anne has come along. She is my assistant here and at home,' Pierre said, tapping the girl lightly on her bottom. She blushed.

By the time I finished my breakfast, the drizzle had turned into a downpour. A walk to the closest bus stop or metro station would get me drenched. A cab was parked along the footpath outside Café the Nice. The driver was probably having his breakfast. Pierre identified him and he agreed to drive me to the Remedes office in Boulogne. It was rush hour in the morning and traffic was unusually heavy. Rain always brought more than the usual number of cars on the roads as walking down to the nearest public transport point became difficult. The taxi moved at a slow pace that turned into a crawl as it reached the Peripherique – the circular road around Paris. The traffic would move a few metres and come to a halt. The taxi driver's patience was wearing thin.

'You need helicopters for this city,' he said.

'You would have equally crowded skies then,' I pointed out.

The man smiled. He suddenly spotted a gap in traffic in the lane to his left and swerved sharply into it. The car coming from behind in that lane honked to a screeching halt. By this time our taxi had covered the length of the gap and had come to a standstill. The car behind us caught up. I looked back. The lady driver was furious. She had put her hands vertically close to her ears as a symbol of horns and what she regarded as the beast-like behaviour of the cabby. He was totally unperturbed and was obviously used to coming across such situations ever so often. Looking at the lady in the rear-view mirror, he shouted, 'Shut up' and that was a summary rejection of her protest. We had hardly made any gain by shifting the lane. However, from my own experience on Paris roads, I knew that it gave you the satisfaction of having done something to get over an otherwise intractable situation. The resulting curses and gestures hurled at each other allowed the drivers to let some of their pent-up steam off.

It was half past nine when I reached my destination. The Remedes office was located in a three-storey building near Bois de Boulogne. Its offices on the front side overlooked a thick green belt. A revolving door led to the foyer where the reception desk was located on the right close to the rear wall. There was an elevator on the left hand side. Against the rear wall, opposite the revolving door, there was a bust of the founder of Remedes on a pedestal, surrounded by a cluster of potted plants. The walls were tastefully decorated with paintings and mural tapestry. The upper floors were equally well done. The Remedes bosses took pride in the fact that they had not degenerated into a modern matter-of-fact office.

Mireille, the receptionist, looked up as I approached her. She was a petite blonde, always impeccably dressed. She had been with the company for over five years now.

'Tiens! Je vous souhaite la bienvenu, Monsieur Khanna,' she welcomed me with a giggle. Claude, the marketing director, had told me that when Mireille joined them, they had found to their annoyance that she could not utter a single sentence without giggling. Over the years, she had learnt to control herself while talking to strangers, but had not changed one bit when it came to talking to colleagues and familiar visitors like me.

'She can giggle through a nuclear holocaust,' Claude would say.

'Is Claude in?' I asked Mireille.

'Not yet. Poor man must be struggling with traffic,' she answered, giggling.

'I guess I'll have to wait,' I said, making myself comfortable on a sofa close to the reception desk.

'So cold. Not a ray of sun. I wish I were in India, Monsieur Khanna.' Mireille, when not attending to the phone or a new arrival, would always engage the waiting visitors in small talk.

'Well the choice is yours at Remedes, Mireille. You people always make me come down here. Why don't you come to India sometimes?'

'O, come on Monsieur Khanna! Even if Remedes were to send people to India, they would send big bosses and not a small fry like me.' A giggle again.

Mireille kept a watchful eye on the main door. Her face lit up as she saw Claude coming in.

'Bonjour, Monsieur. Traffic jam again,' she said.

'What else?' Claude shouted back and then muttered a curse.

Seeing me, he hurried to where I was sitting.

'I am awfully sorry, Lalit. You must have been waiting all this while. I left home early today to be in time for our meeting. But one's punctuality is powerless against our choked roads.'

'I was here at five to nine, Claude. But never mind. What is half an hour's wait among friends,' I said with a poker face.

Claude was even more apologetic, 'Lalit, my apologies once again.'

Mireille giggled. One look at her and Claude saw through my game.

'Lalit, now you better tell me how many seconds before me you arrived.'

'I thought you were my friend, Mireille,' I complained.

'How did you ever think Mireille could keep your gimmick under wraps?' Claude laughed. Turning to Mireille, he asked, 'Has Le General arrived?'

Claude's enquiry was about the Remedes attorney, Maitre Bernard. A big-built man with an impressive moustache and a brisk gait, he was affectionately known in the company as 'Le General'. An amiable man in personal life, he would become impossible once it came to defending the interests of his client. Each time he spoke during business negotiations, words seemed reluctant to leave the security of his mouth and when he finally said something, it was subject to at least five conditions and an equal number of contingencies. There was no way you could get past Bernard. I did not look forward to working with him and yet this is exactly what I would be doing for the next five days. Some agreements with Remedes had come up for renewal and I would be discussing them with Claude and Bernard.

'Le General too must be battling his way on the road somewhere,' Mireille responded to Claude's query. The inevitable giggle followed.

'I hope you had told him about today's meeting.'

'Of course, I did. But his arrival in time was subject to the traffic being normal and the absence of inclement weather.' The giggle was louder than usual this time.

'I am taking Monsieur Khanna to my office. Please send in Le General as soon as he comes.'

Bernard arrived within a few minutes and we got down to business. As expected, the discussions involved a series of hair-splitting arguments. The only respite was a lunch in a nearby restaurant hosted by Claude. Without asking me, he had ordered my favourite Escargots in butter-mint sauce followed by grilled fish fillet and Chablis white wine. Soon after we came back from lunch, there was a phone call from my brother in India. Remedes had offered us a preparation for hypertension. We had been following up clearances at the Indian end. These, my brother said, had come.

'Could you stay on in Paris a little longer to finalise the agreement on this preparation and to familiarse yourself with its manufacturing process?' he asked.

This work, I knew, would take four to five weeks.

'It is fine by me, Udai. But do you realise that if I am unable to complete all this work by the third week of December, I'll be stuck here till the middle of January as nothing will get done during the Christmas-New Year holidays.'

'If you don't mind staying on a little longer in Paris, I don't either,' said Udai, 'but it is important that we get this new production line started at the earliest.'

'As you wish.' I gave in to my elder brother's orders.

The day's work done, I took a metro back from Boulogne. With my mind free of all the business tangles, it went back again to Emilie. Should I make an attempt to meet her? I had a strong urge to call her but was held back by an equally strong voice within me that cautioned me against harking back to the painful past.

I got down at the Charles de Gaulle Etoile station. The place had been appropriately named 'Etoile' or star, as twelve avenues, including the well-known Avenue des Champs Elysees, emanate from this massive roundabout. A leisurely stroll down the Champs Elysees was always refreshing. It was half past five and in any case too early for dinner, which I would take at Café de Nice.

The Etoile was clogged with cars – a common sight at peak traffic hours, with twelve roads disgorging vehicles on to the roundabout. At such moments, the rule of priority to the traffic on your right was forgotten and you had to count on your wits to wade through the jumble of vehicles, avoiding banging into them by inches. I headed away from the Etoile down the Champs Elysees. There were two massive rivers of vehicles moving in both directions on the Avenue. A river of red taillights was visible till the eye could see on the right side of the Avenue, moving towards Place de la Concorde. Another river of yellow anti-fog headlights moving towards Arc de Triomphe could be seen on the other side. Neon signs flashed on both sides of the road. I passed by brightly lit show windows, cinemas and cafés, until I found myself in front of Lido, whose imposing cabaret show had attracted me many times during my visits to Paris. To my right was Avenue George V with its famous Crazy Horse Saloon. I had visited the place for the first time during my apprenticeship with Remedes. I had cut into some other expenses to save money for the show. The financial sacrifice so made was every bit worth it. All the girls dancing at the show were carefully chosen and, in the words of Sunil, 'well proportioned'.

Having some time on my hands, I walked into Café George V and settled down with a coffee in a corner. The place was livening up at that hour with all sorts of people dropping by – tourists, business interlocutors and starry-eyed couples. My gaze fell on a girl sitting at the other end of the café. She had a striking resemblance to Emilie. The same large blue eyes, lovely little nose, thin lips and straight auburn hair falling to her shoulders. I had spent many evenings with Emilie in this Café. Memories were hard to resist.

As I walked down from the Champs Elysees to Café de Nice, I thought of my love for Paris. It had so much to offer – art, architecture, music, theatre, gastronomy, night life ... the list was endless. Above all, I had spent one of the best years of my life in this city. Today I had a strong urge after a long time to reclaim that year. Should I? The strong hesitation was waging a brave battle against the strong urge, but was slowly losing its intensity.

Café de Nice was already full. A TV kept at a high spot in one corner had an old Jean Paul Belmondo movie on. A few police cars chasing bad characters driving at breakneck speed on an auto route. The inevitable came about in a few seconds – two cars crashed into each other with a loud bang and metal flying all around. None of the tables was unoccupied. Pierre emerged from the kitchen.

'Wait a second, Monsieur Khanna. I'll find you a place,' he said as he walked past me to serve a client. By the time he came back, I had occupied a high stool along the bar counter.

'You mind if I have my meal here?' I asked.

'Not at all, Monsieur Khanna. That will give me an opportunity to chat with you while I serve drinks.'

'Good, let's have your suggestions on the menu.'

Café de Nice had a limited choice, different for each meal of course. But Pierre knew my tastes very well.

'I could offer you hot onion soup, followed by Cote d'Agneau. And you must have some Beaujolais Nouveau wine.'

'That would be perfect,' I said.

Pierre passed on my order to Anne, informing her that I liked my Cote d'Agneau well cooked. French onion soup with blobs of melted cheese was my favourite during winter months. Emilie would often make it for me. Emilie again! A long-suppressed obsession was resurfacing.

Anne brought the soup and Pierre served me the wine saying, 'This year it has been superb'.

The release of Beaujolais Nouveau every year is a widely commented upon event in the media – its taste, its prospects and consumers' remarks. The wine comes from the Burgundy region of France. It is a wine made fast to drink and is released with much fanfare on the third Thursday of each November at one minute past midnight – one of the many charming traditions of France!

The meal was delicious. I liked the fruity taste of Beaujolais Nouveau. Some baguette bread and Camembert cheese came gratis. Pierre came by from time to time to ask if I needed anything more. Pierre knew how to pay a little extra attention to his regular customers. He tried to make small talk with me whenever he got a few seconds. My mind, however, was adrift towards a bygone time. I suddenly remembered that I was wearing the same suit as the previous day. My hand impulsively rummaged through the jacket pocket and fished out Sunil's visiting card.

'Can I make a phone call?' I asked Pierre.

'Sure, come inside the kitchen, it's less noisy there.'

Pierre took me to the kitchen and showed me the phone fixed on a wall.

I dialled Emilie's number. The phone kept ringing, but nobody answered.

It was past nine thirty when I returned to Hotel des Alpes. The previous night's receptionist was on duty again.

'All well, I hope, Monsieur,' he smiled, 'otherwise, I could get you another pill.'

'No, that won't be necessary,' I said, 'I don't want to sleep tonight.'

The receptionist was nonplussed for a few seconds and then broke into a smile, 'Is Monsieur expecting a petite amie?' 'Petite amie' being the French expression for sweetheart.

'Yes, I am.'

'Oh,' said the receptionist in an excited voice, 'I shall get her straight to your room, Monsieur.'

'You don't have to bother. She won't come through this entrance,' I said pointing to the main entrance of the hotel.

'She surely won't come through the service entrance?'

'No, not through the service entrance either,' I said as I made my way towards the elevator. Through the corner of my eye, I saw the receptionist shaking his head, partly amazed, partly amused. The man, he must have thought, has gone a little crazy with last night's sleeplessness.

In a few minutes, I was in my bed, my eyes shut but no sign of sleep. Memory lane made an appearance, sharp and clear. In an instant, I was transported to the time when I had first come to France for an apprenticeship with Remedes. I was amazed at the lucidity with which I could recall those days – as if they had remained carefully stored in some unknown vault in the inner reaches of my mind during the intervening years.

I was then around twenty-three. After obtaining a master's degree in chemistry, I was getting ready to work in my father's pharmaceuticals factory. Looking for foreign collaborators, he had signed an agreement with Remedes France SA. Remedes wanted one of us to come to Paris for a year's apprenticeship before we took up the manufacturing of their products in India. Udai was more experienced but was married by then. His first child, Sanjiv, was about a year old. He could not have left his family behind for a year. I was therefore chosen for the apprenticeship. Within the next few weeks, I was in Paris, in a strange environment, not knowing a word of French. I had been given a studio in the suburban area of Boulogne not very far off from the Remedes Headquarters.

Determined to acquire a good understanding of my host country, I took my French classes as seriously as my training with Remedes. My friendship with Sunil had grown. We would often have a drink together after the language classes in a pub named 'Bistro des Artistes'. Every now and then, an Iraqi classmate – his first name was Burhan –would join us. He was much older than us and was training as an automobile engineer with Renault.

After about two weeks into the language course, Sunil told us that Brigitte had gone down south for a month to be with her parents, as her mother was not keeping well. He was therefore available for longer drinking sessions. Bistro des Artistes had a very romantic ambience every evening. Dim lights, lively music and couples lost in each other. Ours was the only all-male group. A few glasses of beer or wine with snacks were our favourite. Burhan, who would preface every sentence with the word 'Brother', usually dominated the conversation. The man was crazy about cars and automobile technology. Drinking sessions with him turned into a monologue on state-of-the-art automobiles. One was exposed to a comparison of the weight, engine power and acceleration capacity of various French, German and Japanese cars. A discourse followed on how lighter bodies of the Japanese cars and their improved aerodynamics shape led to fuel economy. And then the oft-repeated statement, 'Brother, I marvel at the speed modern cars can attain. But for limits of safety, one could do two hundred kilometres an hour.' We were soon convinced that Burhan was not the most exciting company for a relaxed evening. 'We have had enough of Burhan's brotherly affection,' Sunil declared one day, 'Each time he speaks of cars, my patience runs out at two hundred kilometres a second.' A reflective pause and Sunil pronounced,

'What we need old chap is female company.' A fine declaration of intent. All that needed to be done was to implement it and therein lay our problem. Our first thought went to the language class. It was a statistical disaster from our point of view. Just four ladies in a class of fifteen. One of them was an oldish Dutch woman. The remaining three were a Peruvian, a Japanese and an Austrian. None of them knew English. The language course being still in its initial stages, the French of the entire class was elementary.

All that we had picked up by then were commonplace French words such as a chair, a table, a pen, a pencil, a few words of salutations and a few simple phrases to mention one's name and age, etc. Sunil's French was atrocious, to say the least. He had not been able to bring himself to pronounce a single word correctly except for the salutation 'Bon jour'. This did not deter him from forging ahead with his chosen task. He was, after all, a determined soul. Two days later, I reached the class a little late. The teacher was explaining some simple verbs. Sunil looked very pleased with life. He passed on a piece of paper to me on which he had written: 'The Peruvian and the Austrian have agreed to join us for a drink after the class.' I did not know how he had managed it, but was all admiration for his social skills. As soon as the class was over, Sunil asked me to go with the girls to the Bistro as he would take a few minutes to pay some outstanding dues and join us thereafter. The movement plan was explained through gestures to the girls. Burhan was persuaded to lay off for a day. We walked down quietly to the Bistro. Sunil arrived in a few minutes. One look at the girls and he procalimed 'Bonjour' in a loud and crisp voice. The salutation was unnecessary and out of place at that juncture. However, that was the only French word he could pronounce properly and constituted a good beginning. The salutation seemed to emanate from the mouth of a full-blooded Frenchman. The only problem was that having uttered it, Sunil had exhausted his entire vocabulary of the French language. The conversation nonetheless had to be carried forward. Sunil looked at me for sustenance. I taxed my brain but all I could think of were the most inappropriate words for the occasion – a table, a chair, a pen! Drinks were ordered. All that we could do for the next few minutes was to exchange smiles. The two girls also did not have a common language between them. Eventually, gestures were resorted to. As frustration grew, the gestures became more and more vigorous, with hands and arms flying in all directions. This inevitably attracted amused glances from others around. Ours looked like a group of deaf and dumb.

The experiment had been a complete failure. What next? We had no further ideas until Sunil's enterprising spirit prodded him into action again. To my utter astonishment, I found him gesticulating to the Japanese girl before commencement of class two days later. She was a serious looking girl with a deadpan face and did not seem to be someone out for fun. Beggars cannot be choosers, I thought. As he tried to express himself through gestures, Sunil bowed every now and then to ensure the success of his mission. A faint smile appeared on the girl's face and she nodded in acceptance of Sunil's invitation. This time both Burhan and I were asked to lay off. But we followed Sunil and the Japanese girl to the Bistro and installed ourselves in a corner from where we could keep a discreet eye on our friend. What transpired was a repeat of our outing the other day – a series of gestures. The Japanese had a cup of coffee and got up to depart. Much bowing went on as she left. As soon as she was gone, we pounced upon Sunil. 'Hope your back is all right.' I pulled his leg, 'I have never seen you bowing so much earlier.'

'Shut up and mind your own business,' Sunil barked, exasperation writ large on his face.

As we were leaving the Bistro, Burhan added fuel to the fire by asking if we would like to accompany him to an auto show the following day. Sunil gave him one cutting look and shouted a firm 'No'. Burhan went his own way. Sunil was in a reflective mood as we walked down to the metro station. Finally, he broke his silence, 'What we need old chap are English knowing girls.' Another fine declaration of intent. But how were we going to get such tailor-made feminine company? Within a few days, Sunil had a breakthrough and was all excitement.

'You are in for a pleasant surprise in the Bistro this evening, Lalith.' My attempts to make him reveal the secret of his high spirits failed. I could absorb little in the class and finally we were in the dreamy surroundings of Bistro and ordered a beer each.

'Where is your surprise?' I asked.

'Have a little patience, Lalith,' Sunil chided me and beamed as he stood up.

'Ah, there you are.' He greeted two ladies approaching him.

He went through the ritual of kissing their cheeks. In the typical local manner, this form of greeting amounted to a hurried contact of one's cheeks with those of the person one was greeting. However, Sunil's kisses were no hurried affair. They were executed diligently as proper kisses. The scoundrel had his own version of local customs!

'Meet my friend, Lalith. He is from India.' Sunil then turned towards me, 'This is Emilie and her friend Catherine.'

'Hello' Catherine said, extending her hand. Emilie just smiled as she shook hands with me.

The ladies ordered red wine. While they were ordering their drink, Sunil whispered to me, 'Not much scope for me, old chap. Emilie is a distant cousin of Brigitte. But you must act.'

'It's ages since we met the first and the last time. I think it was a get together organised by Emilie,' Sunil told Catherine.

'Yes, it's more than six months. Time flies.'

Catherine, Sunil said, was working in the billing section of the local Hilton hotel. She appeared to be a canny woman, very talkative and fluent in English. She said she had worked for two years with a tour operator before she took up her current job. She had been twice to India with tourist groups and raved about those visits. That's when Emilie spoke up for the first time, 'When I take my next holiday, I would like to go to India.' Catherine took over again – this time about her visit to Sri Lanka where she had spent fifteen glorious days on sunbathed beaches. She then gave us a tour d'horizon of various regions of France.

'Why did you give up your earlier job? You must have been a superb tour guide,' Sunil asked.

'Well, I didn't like travelling all the time.'

Emilie was mostly quiet. In any case, Catherine hardly gave anyone a chance to speak. When Catherine fell silent for a few seconds, I asked Emilie what she did for a living. Before she could answer, Catherine said, 'She is a biochemist and is doing medical research these days to alleviate human suffering.'

I turned to Emilie again, 'And what is the subject of your research?'

'I am with a medical research institute. My team works on Parkinson's disease.'

'So you know who to go to if you ever develop Parkinson's,' Catherine laughed.

'Catherine has a good sense of humour,' Sunil said.

'We have something in common.' I told Emilie, 'I am doing an internship with Remedes France.'She smiled. My repeated attempts to draw her out failed either because she just smiled or answered my queries in monosyllables or because Catherine spoke up before her.

'We must leave now,' Catherine said around nine, 'Tomorrow is a working day.'

'Hope to see both of you again soon,' Sunil said.

'We should certainly not let six months pass before we meet again,' Catherine laughed.

I looked at Emilie. She just extended her hand to both Sunil and me.

'I am sorry if my friend has been a little quiet. She is a very private person, you see. Takes ages to open up,' Catherine said.

'It's perfectly understandable. After all, we obliged Emilie to speak in English. Maybe she is not entirely comfortable with the language,' I found myself coming to Emilie's defence.

After the ladies had left, Sunil turned to me triumphantly and said, 'What do you say? Wasn't it a pleasant surprise? You should focus on Catherine. What a lively girl! You can contact her at the Hilton. This Emilie is so reserved. I have met her a few times with Brigitte and yet she remains so aloof.'

Brigitte had come back and Sunil was all but non-available for our post-class outings. He would once in a while join us for a coffee and then rush back home. Having a drink with Burhan remained as painful as ever. A few outings with him for lack of company had left my head throbbing with details of cars and their engines.

One day I called the Hilton. Catherine was on duty and was put through in a few seconds.

'Catherine, this is Lalit here. I hope you remember me.'

'Of course, I do. I don't forget my friends,' she chuckled.

'Well, I thought we could meet one of these days,' I said.

'Superb idea,' she said. She paused for a second and added, 'Listen, I plan to watch a movie tomorrow. Why don't you join me?'

'Which movie?' I enquired.

'It's a French movie, starring Louis de Funes, called *Le Gendarme en balade*.'

'I may not be able to follow much,' I said.

'You don't have to when it's a Louis de Funes comedy. Besides, I shall explain the story to you.'

'That would be lovely. Where do we meet?'

Catherine gave me the name of a cinema near the Champs Elysees.

We were there a few minutes before the movie started. Catherine told me about Louis de Funes. He hailed from a Spanish family, worked as a pianist and in theatre before becoming a film actor. He became a major film star at the age of 49. That's why in his popular films; he appeared as a middle-aged or old man.

Catherine had been right. I enjoyed the film despite not knowing much French. The comical actions of Louis de Funes transcended the language barrier. Catherine leaned every now and then to whisper the gist of dialogues in my ear. Each time she did so, she left me with the pleasant whiff of the subtle perfume she was wearing. She laughed her guts out. On a few occasions, when the scene was too funny, she clutched my arm out of excitement. She was obviously a woman out for fun.

After the movie, I invited her to a nearby café for a drink. Our conversation centred on the film. We couldn't control our laughter remembering some of the scenes.

'Hope you are enjoying your stay in Paris?' Catherine asked.

'You bet I am. It's such a lively city.'

'And it's also very romantic,' Catherine added.

'Yes it is.'

'The love of many famous couples blossomed here,' she said with a smile.

'You have a lovely smile,' I said.

'Really. All my friends say so,' Catherine said in a tone of excitement.

'Have you been around the city?' she asked.

'Yes, I have seen a few famous landmarks.'

'Let me take you to some more interesting places in the coming weeks,' she said.

'Such as?'

'Such as a theatre.'

'I would love to go to a theatre, but language may be a problem,' I said.

'Not so long as you have a competent interpreter in me,' Catherine said.

'You are so kind.'

'It's just that I am beginning to like your company.'

'So when do we meet next?' I asked.

'Let me check what is on in theatres and I'll call you.'

'Au revoir, Catherine,' I said.

'Why don't you call me Cathie? That's what I like my friends to call me,' she said.

'Au revoir, Cathie.'

'Au revoir, Lalit.'

The next day, when I met Sunil in the language class, I told him about my outing with Catherine.

'Good,' he said, 'and what did you do after the movie?'

'Well we had a drink together at a café.'

'And then?' he asked.

'Then we parted company.'

'God!' he banged his fist on the desk in front of him, 'How could you do that?'

'Do what?'

'You should have invited her to your place for a drink.'

'Why?'

'Well, you don't want me to spell out everything for you. Do you?'

'Why not?' I asked.

'Because as a matter of principle, I don't interfere in the personal affairs of others.'

'You just did that to me,' I said.

'I just gave you some sound advice,' said Sunil with a disarming smile.

He was quiet for a few seconds and then said, 'Now next time you go out with her, don't forget to invite her to your place for a drink afterwards. The crucial moment is when you finish with whatever you have taken her out for – a film or a meal. That's when you must act quickly.'

'But I don't know her well so far. I find her too boisterous for me,' I protested.

'I am not asking you to establish a lifelong relationship with her. Just enjoy yourself and move on,' Sunil was ready with an answer.

I kept quiet. There was no point in arguing with him.

Catherine called me a few days later. She said she had managed two seats for Moliere's *Le Malade Imaginaire* at the Studio-Theatre of Comedie Francaise the following Friday. The tickets had to be picked up the next day and she would do so.

'No, you must tell me where to pick up the tickets,' I said.

'Well, it will be much easier if I do so,' she said.

'No, I insist on doing so,' I said.

She gave me the details and we agreed to meet at the theatre.

I had read the English translation of *Le Malade Imaginaire* and therefore enjoyed the play. Comedie Francaise was founded by a decree of Louis XIV in 1680, Catherine informed me. It was closed down during the French revolution in 1793 and reopened in 1799 at Salle Richelieu made available by the new government. Today Comedie Francaise has three theatres in Paris – Salle Richelieu, Theatre de Vieux-Colombier and the Studio-Theatre. Catherine also told me that Le Malade Imaginaire, centring on Argan, the hypochondriac, was the last work of Moliere. It had first been performed in 1673, the year Moliere died.

Once the play was over, the crucial 'Sunilian moment' had arrived and I was mustering courage to invite Catherine over to my place for a drink. But before I could say anything, she said, 'Why don't you join me for a drink at my place? I have some food lying over in the fridge and that should be good enough for our dinner.'

'Thanks. That's so nice of you,' I said.

'You don't have to be so formal,' said Catherine.

We took a metro to Catherine's place.

'Don't mind if you find my studio in a mess,' Catherine said while opening the front door.

She was right. The studio was indeed in a mess. Clothes, magazines and other items strewn all over. Catherine hurriedly cleared the three-seater sofa lying along a wall and asked me to take a seat. It was bitterly cold. She took out a bottle of Cognac and we quickly downed two drinks each.

'A quick third one,' she proposed.

'No, let's have the third one slowly,' I said.

'Ok, then why don't you pour yourself and me a drink,' she said.

As I was pouring the drink, Catherine flung away her pullover, saying she was feeling hot and opened the top two buttons of the loose shirt she was wearing underneath.

'Let me show you some pictures of my visits to India,' she said. She dug out an album from a table in a corner piled up with various things, got a bowl full of nuts from the kitchen and sat down to my right on the sofa – almost leaning on me.

She opened the album, placing one half of it on my thigh and the other half on hers and started showing the photos to me with her characteristic flourish. Catherine in Goa, frolicking in the sea with friends, lazing around on the beach, visiting a temple, visiting churches in Old Goa. The scene then shifted – Catherine in front of the Qutab Minar, Catherine at the Lal Quila, Catherine riding an elephant, Catherine at a party by a French friend living in Delhi, Catherine in front of the Taj Mahal, Catherine in the pink city of Jaipur, etc. etc.

This was my second outing with Catherine and I still was not decided on what kind of association I wanted with her. But I was coming to the end of my third drink of Cognac and alcohol had dimmed my discretion. I was not in full control of myself. I found myself staring at Catherine every now and then as she continued showing me the photographs. Her shirt had slipped off her left shoulder. It seemed as if events had followed a script written by Sunil. His words – 'Enjoy yourself' – were ringing in my ears.

We had reached the last page of the album, which had a picture of Catherine with a subtle smile, which she said had been taken in a very old style photo studio in Jaipur.

'I love your smile. I just love it,' I said.

'Then why don't you kiss it,' Catherine said, looking at me with a smile.

'May I?' I asked.

'Lalit! If you ask me that question each time you want to kiss me, we will end up wasting a lot of time,' she said with a laugh.

I bent over to kiss her, but before I could do so, the phone rang.

'Merdre,' Catherine cursed under her breath as she got up to take the call.

The phone conversation was at first calm but cold. 'I am well', 'Yes all is well' – I could understand her saying. But then the conversation turned into a heated argument. Catherine was hysterical and was shouting at the person at the other end. I could snatch only a few words and a name – Giovanni. Finally, Catherine banged the phone and screamed as if to no one in particular, 'I have had enough of him. How can he do this to me? He wants to come and spend a few days with me, but is not willing to leave the other woman.'

She then walked up to the sofa, almost fell on it, this time leaning completely on me, put her head on my shoulder, covered her face with her hands and cried uncontrollably. I did not know how to react. I put my arm around her shoulders to comfort her. She took a few minutes to recover, wiped her tears off with her hands and said, 'I am so sorry. I lost control of myself.'

'Don't worry,' I said.

'Would you have another drink?' she asked.

'No,' I said.

She snuggled upto me and smiled. I turned my face away.

'You seem to be bored,' she said.

'No, it's just that I have a headache and must go home to take rest,' I said.

'Hah, that's a woman's excuse,' she said, 'but I shall let it pass.'

I got up, put on my overcoat, said goodbye and left.

Sunil's script had gone horribly wrong somewhere.

It was ten days since my last meeting with Catherine. I had not called her; nor had she called me. Her hyper demeanour, I thought, was incompatible with my sober nature. And now there was this mystery of a certain Giovanni, who was unknown to me. Her friend Emilie had shown no interest in meeting me. Finally it was out of sheer loneliness that I called Catherine.

'Cathie,' I said.

'Lalit!!!' she almost screamed, 'How nice to hear your voice. I am awfully sorry for the other day.'

'Well you don't have to be sorry.'

'It's just that I was too upset,' she said.

'Well, forget about that day,' I tried to put her at ease and added, 'I thought we could have a meal together one of these days.'

'Marvellous idea, but I am going to be terribly busy for the next two days,' she said.

'That shouldn't be a problem. I have in mind lunch the coming Saturday. Hope you will be free.'

'Let me see.' She reflected for a moment and then said, 'That's fine. I have nothing lined up that day. Where do we meet?'

I mentioned the name of a restaurant close to the Opera that one of the Remedes colleagues had recommended.

'What time?'

'Let's meet around twelve,' I said.

'Ok. I shall be there.'

Before I could say anything further, Catherine asked, 'And how is your French since we last met.'

'Oh, that was only ten days ago. I am more or less where I was that day.'

'That's normal. You can practise your French with me every now and then. That would help,' she said.

'But your English is so good and that leaves me no incentive to speak French. I...er...was wondering if Emilie too would like to join us for lunch on Saturday.'

There was a pause and then Catherine enquired, 'Why? Is Sunil joining us?'

'No he won't be coming. But I just thought it would be nice if Emilie...'

'I hope you are not one of those men who want a harem around,' Catherine had a hearty laugh.

'Inviting two ladies together for lunch does not make up a harem,' I protested.

On the other hand, Catherine's curiosity was natural. I had not been able to give a convincing reason for inviting Emilie to a lunch which Catherine thought was for her. I was at a loss for words but was spared the need to say something as Catherine said, 'I shall check with Emilie and bring her along if she is free.'

Something within me hoped Emilie would come.

It was the first week of December. The whole of Friday night, it snowed heavily. There was a thick layer of snow on the roads in the morning. This being my first experience of a snowfall, I did not know how long it would take for normal traffic to resume. However, the cleaning of roads started quickly and by eleven, some cars made an appearance. I took a metro to the restaurant and reached there at the appointed hour. The place was practically empty. I ordered a drink. Slowly other customers started trickling in, but there was no sign of my invitees. Finally, Catherine walked in, half an hour late and all alone.

'Hello there,' I greeted her. 'Isn't Emilie joining us?'

Catherine looked a little annoyed at my query.

'My dear friend, but for your generous invitation to Emilie, I would have been here dot on time. She had some work at her institute, but had promised to join me by eleven thirty to accompany me here. And at twelve, she called and asked me to go ahead alone. She is stuck with some urgent task and will join us, if she can, later.'

'Should we wait?' I asked.

'I don't think so.' Catherine shrugged her shoulders.

She ordered an aperitif and launched forth into a monologue on her work, the weather, winter tourist spots in France and much more. Just when I had given up hope of Emilie joining us, I heard a soft 'Bonjour', looked up and was thrilled to see Emilie. Catherine looked irritated.

'Mademoiselle, you ought to know that others' time is also precious. You first made me wait for so long at home, then asked me to go ahead alone and then turned up here within twenty minutes of my arrival.'

'Let's focus on some good food,' I said with a broad smile in an attempt to change the topic.

'I hope you won't do this to me again.' Catherine was not willing to be deprived of the last word. Emilie smiled and that put an end to the unpleasant talk.

The waiter brought the menu card. Emilie said she didn't want an aperitif and ordered grilled chicken with French fries. Catherine ordered a plate of cold cuts, followed by a lamb dish. I asked Emilie to choose a wine. She passed on the task to Catherine, who chose one of the more expensive wines. Her speed of consumption ensured that she cornered most of the wine (a second bottle had to be ordered) and, of course, as usual most of the conversation. By the time we approached the end of our meal she was fairly inebriated.'Eh Lalit, I like your thick black hair. It's just like Giovanni's.' I stared at her.

'Giovanni. Don't you know him? Of course, you don't. I didn't tell you about him the other day. He was assistant manager in our hotel. Got me the job. We lived together for two years before he went back to Rome to take up work there.'

I didn't know how to react. Emilie looked a little embarrassed. Catherine, however, was bent upon talking about her personal life.

'Giovanni was such a marvellous person. I was madly in love with him and then this wretched former girl friend of his resurfaced and lured him back to Italy. I feel so lonely, but I must choose the right guy before I settle down again.'

Emilie whispered something in Catherine's ear.

'Why should I stop?' Catherine shot back, 'I'll do what I want with my life. I must look out for a nice person.' And then she faced me and said, 'Why don't you try your luck, Lalit?'

Emilie blushed and again whispered something to Catherine.

'Is it common for couples to stay together without getting married?' I asked Catherine, more to change the subject than to elicit an answer which, having stayed in France for some time, I knew by then.

'Yes it is becoming more and more common,' said Catherine. 'It gives you complete freedom. You live with the person you love without the responsibility of bringing up a family. You live a life full of fun and can, of course, change your companion whenever you wish to.'

'Just as Giovanni changed his,' I felt like saying but held myself back.

'I don't agree with Catherine,' it was Emilie this time. 'You can enjoy a few years of your life while you are young. But when you get old, you need a family and children to look after you. Besides if everyone thinks like Catherine, there will be no children to secure the future of this country.'

'Hah! You talk like politicians,' Catherine again took over. 'What can children do for their old parents these days?

You and I are in Paris. What do we do for our parents living elsewhere?'

'Well, my mother can always count on me in case of need,' said Emilie.

'You will always remain your mama's baby,' Catherine mocked Emilie.

I interjected to break the course of conversation that had again entered troubled waters, 'I didn't know you spoke English so well, Emilie.'

'I spent a year studying the language in England. And many of our researchers are English speaking.'

There was a pause and I didn't want the conversation to relapse again into something contentious. Fortunately, the waiter came to take orders for dessert. Emilie and I ordered small tarts. Catherine ordered a large helping of ice cream with mixed fruit topping.

Catherine once again monopolised the conversation. It was past two thirty. Many clients at the restaurant were still at varying stages of their meal. Eating out is a favourite pastime in France. Meals in restaurants, especially on holidays, can be a leisurely affair, lasting two to three hours – beginning with an aperitif and an hors d'oeuvre, followed by the main dish accompanied by wine, dessert or cheese and ending with tea/coffee/ liqueur. The waiter, I noticed, had handed over the liqueur card to Catherine.

'Would you take some liqueur?' Catherine asked Emilie.

'No, thanks. I don't need anything more.'

'I shall have an espresso,' I said.

'And I shall have a Cointreau,' declared Catherine.

I wasn't familiar with French liqueurs those days.

'Do you know, Cointreau comes from my home town, Angers?' Catherine said looking at me.

'I didn't know that. In fact, I have never tasted it.'

'Then you must. It's made using orange peels and is named after the family that founded its distillery in the 19th century.'

'Where is Angers?' I asked.

'It is south-west of Paris, about three hours' drive. My parents live there. That reminds me, I'll be visiting them in a week's time. Why don't you come over the next weekend?' Catherine asked. 'You can stay at a reasonably priced pension. Angers is a fabulous place.'

I knew nothing about Angers and had no particular desire to visit it. However an offer had been made and I didn't consider it polite to turn it down outright.

'I would love to visit Angers. Let me see if I can make it.'

Our meal had come to an end. Catherine reiterated her invitation to visit Angers.

'See you sometime,' Emilie said as she left. She had been a little more open than the first time, but still somewhat withdrawn, still an enigma.

It had been a tiring day with a grilling schedule at Remedes and preparation in the evening for a French test the following day. I took a few minutes off late in the evening to toss an omelette by way of dinner. The phone rang.

'Hello ... Is this Lalit ... Lalit, this is Cathie here.'

'Oh, hello Cathie.'

'I hope you are coming to Angers.'

'Well, I haven't been able to give much thought to the visit,' I said. The fact was that I had given no thought whatsoever to Catherine's invitation to visit Angers.

'Oh come on Lalit. You can surely spare two-three days. Giovanni accompanied me to Angers a number of times. He just loved the place.'

Giovanni again? Why must I be dragged into Giovanni's shoes? I was annoyed at Catherine treating me as a successor to this character I had never set my eyes on. I had half a mind of telling her that I was unable to visit Angers. But before I could do so, Catherine spoke up, 'Look if you cannot make it this time, you could come around Christmas when I shall spend a longer time in Angers. I am going this time for a few days only because my parents want Emilie over. She won't be able to come with me for Christmas as she will be visiting her mother then.'

So Emilie was also going to be in Angers. Suddenly Catherine's invitation began to arouse my interest.

'Cathie, I shall try my best to come for a day or two. Give me your parents' phone number and I shall be in touch.'

'Now you are being a good boy and remember you can always visit me again around Christmas.'

'Thanks.'

Remedes had three old Renault 4L cars that were used to ferry their middle-level personnel and papers from the Head Office to their factory. The administrative officer had told me that I could get one of these cars over weekends for my use. I had an international driving licence. My enquiry revealed that two of the cars were in a garage for repairs and the third one would be available only on Sunday. I rang up Catherine. She agreed that a day trip by car would be too tiring and it might be better to travel by train and spend at least two days in Angers. On a second thought, she said it would be good if I could come on a day trip on Sunday. Emilie and she were coming back to Paris on Sunday evening and they could travel back with me. So a day trip was agreed to. I needed company on my outward journey and someone to share driving with me. Sunil agreed to come along as Brigitte was going to be busy with some friends.

It was past twelve when we reached Angers. Situated on the banks of the Maine River, this beautiful city is the historical capital of the Anjou region and gateway to the Loire valley. The girls met us at the appointed spot in front of the Mayor's office. After a hurried meal at a restaurant, we set about to see the city. It was clear that given the time at our disposal, we would not be able to see much. So we asked Catherine to suggest one or two main spots of tourist interest. One place not to be missed, she said, was Chateau du Roi Rene. With seventeen round towers marking its perimeter, the castle traces its origins to the 13th century. It was extensively renovated in the 15th century by Prince Rene who ruled the region. Hence its name. Catherine, the former tourist guide, took over. History behind each and every stone was explained. We saw the statue of Rene by the famous 19th century sculptor, David d'Angers. Talking of the sculptor, Catherine said, 'Angers is known for three great personalities: Rene, David d'Angers and the third one is of course none other than your friend Catherine d'Angers.' Everyone had a hearty laugh.

'You ought to be a little modest,' Emilie said.

'I know I need to be not only a little but much more modest. But you know equally well that I won't change. I am what I am.' One could not fault Catherine for lack of candidness.

In the castle, we visited the gallery of tapestries, dating from the 14th century, that tells the story of the Apocalypse.

'These tapestries depict not only the theme of Apocalypse but also aspects of the political and social life of the region at the end of the 14th century when these were made. Only 70 of the original 100 have survived and together add up to the impressive length of more than 100 metres,' Catherine explained.

We had some more time and, on Catherine's advice, decided to visit yet another landmark – the Saint Maurice Cathedral.

The walk from the Chateau to the cathedral took us through the medieval quarter of Angers. It was a treat to walk in the narrow cobblestone streets.

'The Cathedral,' Catherine explained, 'was built by two bishops of Angers: Normand de Doue and Guillaume de Beaumont. It's a mixture of Romanesque and Gothic architecture. It has a Romanesque nave, an Angevin vaulting and a Gothic transept.'

We saw some exquisite stained glass windows in the cathedral, particularly the one in the transept depicting the life of Saint Julien.

'Catherine, Angers is every bit the wonderful place you described it as. I wish we could have stayed here longer. Maybe some other time,' I said. The short time spent in the city had convinced me of its charms.

'Well, you have to thank me for bringing you here. And you have my invitation to come here again,' said Catherine.

'I would love to,' I said.

We picked up the girls' baggage from Catherine's home and set off for Paris around five in the evening. Sunil had done most of the driving on our way to Angers. So the return journey came to my share. It was pitch dark and extremely cold. Catherine chattered for some time but was soon overpowered by the snug interior of the car and dozed off. In a few minutes, Sunil and Emilie were also asleep. I was the only unfortunate being forced to stay awake. I reflected on the two girls in the rear seat. Catherine was attractive, very lively and evidently out for fun. But she was too hyper for my liking and clearly still emotionally involved with Giovanni. Emilie too was very attractive and I loved her maturity and gentle manner. But she remained a mystery. She had given me little indication of what she thought of me. In fact, she had spoken very little to me or perhaps had not been given much time by Catherine to speak. How long would it take me to get to know her? I was getting impatient.

Everyone woke up as we reached the outskirts of Paris.

'Old chap, you drop me at the nearest metro station on entering the city and we must ask the ladies for their address so that you could drop them at their home,' Sunil said.

I did not like the thought of bringing the evening to such an abrupt end and parting company with Emilie so soon. God only knew when I would meet her again. Some more time with her might enable me to unravel her mysterious demeanour.

'Why don't we go to the Bistro for a drink and snack? I wonder if anyone of us would have the energy to cook dinner,' I said.

'Excellent idea. I would hate to go home and cook a meal at this time,' Catherine agreed.

The issue was settled and we landed up at the Bistro. Drinks and snacks having been ordered, I went to the jukebox to register a request for the Neil Diamond song 'Play Me' that was a rage those days. 'You are the Sun, I am the moon, you are the words, I am the tune, Play Me' – I loved the lyrics. The song came on and then suddenly something went wrong with the music system and it fell silent. The cacophony of the clients' chatter, usually drowned by music, surfaced. Catherine was making a point to Sunil and Emilie was listening to her. My disinterest in her talk took the better of me and I started whistling the 'Play Me' tune while looking at the busy street outside through the pub window. In a few seconds, I turned to find Emilie staring at me. I stopped whistling. Catherine was still busty talking to Sunil.

'Please whistle the tune again. I love this song,' Emilie said.

My heart leapt. It was a moment of both joy and surprise. I controlled my emotions and whistled the tune.

'Again please. It's lovely.'

When I was whistling the tune a third time, Catherine caught up with what was happening. She had a part amused, part annoyed look on her face and said, 'Hey, what's going on here. Is it a whistle concert?'

'This talent of yours was hidden from me too, Lalith,' Sunil said.

Before I could say anything, the Bistro music system came on.

'I was merely filling in for the music system,' I said.

'We can ask them to switch it off permanently. You can whistle tunes for their clients and make some money in the process,' Sunil pulled my leg.

'I strongly support you. He can whistle the tunes so well,' Emilie told Sunil.

Catherine looked away.

It was time to break up. Sunil said he would take the metro home.

'Why don't you drop Emilie off first and then drive me home,' Catherine suggested as we drove off.

'That would mean retracing a long distance. Emilie's house is closer to mine,' I said.

Catherine kept quiet. She could not question my logic. She said a rather formal 'Au revoir' as she got off in front of her apartment block.

Emilie did not speak much as we drove to her place. When she got off the car, I too came out to say goodbye. She looked up and I bent down to kiss her cheeks in a local style goodbye. Before I could reach her cheek, she extended her lips and I kissed her.

'When would I see you next?' I asked.

'I don't know. I shall be going to visit my mother in a few days. Maybe when I come back.'

'That would be too long,' I complained.

'Let's keep in touch,' she said with a warm smile.

'Give me your phone number.'

'Sure,' she said as I proceeded to jot down the number.

I drove off. She stood waving goodbye.

The next morning I got up, utterly pleased with life in the knowledge that the mysterious veil around Emilie had finally lifted somewhat. During the day, the pleasure turned into a consuming desire to see her again. I somehow controlled myself till the evening and phoned her.

'Hello Emilie.'

'Hello, Lalit,' she chuckled.

'I have been thinking of you the whole day.'She laughed.

'Emilie, I want to see you.'

'But we met only yesterday.'

'Please understand. I need to see you.'

'You must learn to be patient,' she was out to tease me.

'I am a patient person by nature, but realised today that I am very different when it comes to my yearning to meet you.'

'I am so sorry to have ruined your patience.'

'Emilie, tell me when can I see you again.'

'I told you I shall be visiting my mother in a few days and we can meet when I come back.'

'And I told you that would be too long.'

'Good lord, I didn't mean to cause such agony to a friend.'

'But you have.'

'All right, let's meet day after.'

'Why not tomorrow?'

'I have dinner at a colleague's place tomorrow.'

'Okay, let's meet day after. Where?'

Emilie suggested a café near her house.

'Great. Shall we make it around six?' I asked.

'Six thirty would be better.'

'Thanks. Look forward to seeing you.'

'Me too.'

I had registered some further progress.

I had been at the café near Porte de Saint Cloud for a few minutes when Emilie walked in.

'Bon Soir.'

'Bon Soir, Emilie,' I extended my hand.

'How are you?'

'I have been awful.'

'Why?' Emilie was concerned.

'Because I couldn't see you for two days.'

'Now that sounds serious.'

'You bet it is.'

'Monsieur, dame. Bon Soir.' The waiter was there to take our order.

'Bon Soir. I'll have an espresso,' Emilie said.

'And a glass of red wine for me please.'

The waiter was gone.

'Catherine called me yesterday and wanted to know if you had been in touch with me,' Emilie said.

'What did you tell her?'

'I told her I was going to meet you today.'

'What did she say?'

'She said nothing. But I guess she was disappointed. She has been...er.... sort of interested in you.'

'She is a nice girl but not my kind.'

'What kind of girl would you like?'

'Someone like you.'

'Ooh la la! It's getting too serious.' Emilie giggled.

I looked squarely into her eyes and said, 'I told you it's very serious. Emilie, I am in love with you.'

'Good lord! It's been so quick.'

'It's been quicker than I ever imagined.'

'You sound like a character out of a fairy tale.'

'Right now I feel I am living a fairy tale full of happiness.'

'You are such a romantic, Lalit.'

'Yes, I am. Would you like me to be any different?'

'No. I like you as you are.'

'Thank God, you like me as I am.'

'Tell me something more about yourself.'

'I am younger of the two children of my parents. We live in Delhi and have a pharmaceuticals factory there. Perhaps I told you earlier that I am doing an apprenticeship with Remedes France SA and will be here until August next year.'

'I have heard so much about India. It's such a mysterious country for us in many ways. I would love to go there.'

'You should come next year when I am back.'

'That would be great.'

'Now tell me something about you,' I asked.

'I am the only child of my mother. She lives in Poitiers. As you know, I work in a medical research institute. I am sure you will get to know more about me as we go along.'

'I am sure I will. I am in no hurry. But tell me why you remained such an enigma during our previous meetings? You hardly spoke,' I said.

'You know it's difficult for anyone to talk when Catherine is around. Besides, she seemed to be interested in you and I didn't wish to let her down.'

'Aren't you letting her down now?'

'No. I have not been disloyal to my friend. What is happening now is the result of your choice,' Emilie laughed stressing the word 'your'.

'I hope Catherine won't be too upset.'

'No, I am sure she would be all right. She is a little boisterous, but a very fine human being. She has been feeling very lonely since Giovanni left her all of a sudden. I hope she finds someone interesting soon.'

'I would be happy if she did.'

'Lalit, can I ask you to whistle the "Play Me" tune again.'

'With pleasure,' I said and proceeded to whistle the tune.

'You know I am also a fan of Neil Diamond,' Emilie said.

'Are you? We are already beginning to find things we share.'

'*Play Me* and *Sweet Caroline* are two of my favourite songs.'

'I love *Sweet Caroline*.'

'The lyrics are so lovely: Sweet Caroline, good times never seemed so good.'

'In fact, right now I could say: Sweet Emilie, good times never seemed so good,' I said.

'You must not rush into such statements before you know me well. You said you were not in a hurry.'

'I am not in a hurry, but I also know well what I feel right now. I know you well enough to say that good times never seemed as good as at this moment.'

'You are an incorrigible romantic.'

'I told you I am.'

'I must leave now,' Emilie said looking at her watch.

'Why not have dinner together?'

'No, I must go. My mother is going to call me at home at eight.'

I wanted to ask if I could accompany her home. But she had not invited me to and I did not wish to impose myself.

'When do we meet again?'

'I knew your perennial question was coming,' Emilie chuckled.

'I hope I'll get a good answer.'

'Well, I am going to Poitiers the coming Saturday to be with my mother for Christmas and will be back on the 28th. Let's meet when I am back.'

'There are still two days between now and Saturday.'

'Sometimes I wonder how you spent your time before you met me?'

'But I didn't know you then.'

'Our office is organising a Christmas dinner day after. Would you like to join me?'

'I would love to.'

'I shall call to tell you the time and place.'

We left the café and walked a short distance to a turning from where we were to go different ways. It was extremely cold and there were very few people on the streets.

I kissed her goodbye.

'Why didn't you kiss me when I came to the café?' Emilie asked.

'It would have been awkward with so many people looking on,' I said.

'No one minds it here,' Emilie giggled.

'Then let me kiss you again.'

Another kiss and she was gone.

The Christmas dinner had been organised at Emilie's research institute. She introduced me to their director who was personally receiving all the guests.

'Very pleased to meet you. Please enjoy yourself. I shall catch up with you later on,' he said hurriedly in perfect English as he turned to receive the next guest in the reception line.

The guests were seated on tables of six each. It was still the time for drinks and a buffet would be served later on. A tall and tastefully decorated Christmas tree added to the charm of the evening. Emilie had made sure that we were seated on a table where everyone knew English. We got ourselves some red wine. The remaining persons on our table included two men and two women. One of them, Gerard Sambrana, was particularly fluent in English. He was the head of Emilie's research team and had lived in England for a long time.

Christmas carols were being sung when we joined the party. A group in one corner led the singing and all guests added their voice. The tunes were familiar to me, but the words in French were largely unfamiliar.

'This must all be so new to you,' said one of the ladies when the singing stopped.

'Not really. We have a large number of Christians in India. I have many Christian friends and am quite familiar with Christmas festivities,' I said.

'I believe you have a large number of Muslims also,' said the other lady.

'We have a Hindu majority and a large Muslim minority, Christians, Sikhs, Buddhists, Jews – people belonging to different faiths.'

'That must be a big problem – managing a country with people of so many faiths. One reads every now and then about communal violence in India,' said the first lady.

'We regard our religious diversity as strength and not a problem. Unfortunately, violence in the name of religion has also been a fact of life,' I said.

'That's not the misfortune of your country alone. The history of mankind is replete with instances of killing and brutality perpetrated by adherents of different religions. I wonder if religions have served any purpose other than pushing people into obscurantist beliefs and making them intolerant to the point of cruelty and barbaric conduct.' It was Sambrana.

'No one can deny the existence of violence in the name of religions, but I would not make a sweeping statement against religions like you. In any case, religion for me is not bigoted belief. It's a direct relationship between my God and me. It's a faith that does not exclude the right of others to have faith in their own way in the Creator,' I said.

'That is if there is a Creator,' Sambrana said in a mocking tone that was provocative.

'How can you doubt the existence of God? Who has created this complex universe? Who has created life? You and I cannot create life.' I was not going to let Sambrana get away with his outrageous remark.

'The frontiers of science are expanding fast. The mysteries of the universe are unravelling. A day will come when we will be able to create life in a laboratory. We are slowly getting to grips with the origins of life. You must be aware of the laboratory experiments that simulated pre-biotic environment on earth and showed that the coming together of certain chemical substances by chance, aided by ultraviolet radiation and lightning, would have given rise to the building blocks of life that evolved over billions of years to the complex life that we see today.'

'You seem to prefer calling God by the name "chance". It is inconceivable that the complex existence around us would have come about without a hand guiding it – call it God or chance. When you say that the frontiers of science are expanding, you acknowledge that there is a territory beyond these frontiers. And it is a vast territory that remains unexplored. If human mind is to grapple with this uncharted zone, religion and faith must take over where science ends. You must also not forget that religions have provided norms of orderly social interaction at various stages of human history.'

'Secular norms of social conduct have been as effective, if not more, as the norms prescribed by religions and certainly more inclusive and non-discriminatory,' Sambrana persisted. 'We should wait for the light of science to illuminate the dark territory beyond its reach today. The fact that there is a terrain yet to be explained by science does not mean that we fill it with illogical thoughts such as existence of a Supreme Being. Let me see where we all stand on this. Those of you, who believe in the existence of God, please raise your hands.'

Four of us other than Emilie and Sambrana raised our hands.'I would not go as far as Gerard, but in my view, a final word is yet to be said on the existence of God and it may perhaps never be said,' Emilie said.

'I can only reiterate what I said earlier. Religion must begin where science ends. Otherwise, how would we deal with the inexplicable phenomena around us?' I said in a firm tone.

'Such as?' Sambrana asked.

'Such as death. What happens when a person dies?'

'There is no need to weave a web of obscurity around phenomena such as death. Life is a biological balance of various chemical substances occurring in nature. When this balance is disturbed beyond redemption, death takes place.'

'I wonder if human mind can be at peace with such cold logic,' I said.

'Why not?'

'It takes away from the beauty of life. It seeks to reduce human beings to machines. It leaves no room for charming aspects of life such as human feelings and emotions,' I said.

'Life is beautiful and must be lived to the full. But it need not be turned into a mystery. The emotions and feelings that you talk of are all the result of chemical and electrical signals flowing through the human brain whose complexities are also getting unravelled.' Sambrana was unflinching.

'How uninteresting,' I said.

The director of the institute had walked up to our table.

'What's going on here?' he asked.

'Gerard is at his atheistic best as usual,' said one of the women.

'Oh no! Not again. Not today of all the days when we are celebrating a religious festival. For God's sake, leave aside your atheism for today, Gerard. The table is laid. Let our friends help themselves to some food,' the director said.

'Cut out "For God's sake" from your appeal and I shall cut out my atheism for today,' said Sambrana.

Everyone had a hearty laugh as we made our way to the buffet.

The following week was a period of agonising wait for Emilie. Work at Remedes had come to a virtual standstill because of Christmas vacations. I was unable to concentrate on whatever little I was required to do. Sunil had joined Brigitte at her parents' home for Christmas. Even Burhan was not available to sermonise me on automobiles as he had gone back to Iraq to visit his family. I visited the Bistro alone every evening and drank more than my usual quota. It was a pleasant feeling to be in love, laced with the pain of separation.

A strange sense of loneliness gnawed at me. Some colleagues at Remedes were still around and the working day was spent with them. Paris was as lively as ever and yet I was lonely because the lady I loved was not around. A few short calls to Emilie at her mother's place in Poitiers were the only respite.

Emilie was expected back by lunchtime on the 28th. However, my repeated calls at her home did not elicit an answer till the evening. Finally, I called her mother's number. Emilie answered.

'How come you are not back?' I asked.

'My mother has been unwell since yesterday. We went to the doctor this morning. He said it's nothing serious, but she needs rest for a day or two. So I have decided to stay a little longer.'

'When would you be back?'

'My mother wanted me to stay on for the New Year's Eve, but I am keen to be in Paris for that. I should be back the day after evening.'

'Listen, have you planned New Year's Eve?' I asked.

'Well, a group of friends from my institute are planning to spend it in a restaurant. But I haven't yet decided to join them.'

'Would you please accept my invitation to spend New Year's Eve with me?'

'That would be lovely.' Emilie's response made my day.

'Where would you like to go?'

'Don't go in for one of the big places. They are quite expensive and may already be fully booked. Choose any small restaurant.' Emilie advised.

The newspapers were full of dinner-dance ads of restaurants for the New Year's Eve. I was able to get a table at the restaurant to which I had invited Emilie and Catherine the other day. Remedes obliged by giving me a car for the evening.

It had snowed repeatedly over the last week of December. Temperatures had remained in the range of -10 to -15. I picked up Emilie from her apartment block. She had a gift-wrapped package in her hand. She saw me looking at it and said, 'That's a surprise for you, but you can see it only after we reach the restaurant.'

'I have a surprise for you too. Maybe you would now agree to come out with our respective surprises right away,' I said.

'No, let's wait till we reach the restaurant,' Emilie said.

'As you wish.'

A part of the restaurant had been cleared to create a dance floor. Our table was not too far from this area.

'Let me see the surprise you have for me.' I was dying to see the gift she had brought along.

'No, you must first reveal your surprise,' Emilie said.

I gave her the small gift-wrapped packet I had in my pocket.'This is your Christmas gift. A little late. Hope you like it.'

'O! I love it, Thank you!' It was an Yves Saint Laurent Rive Gauche perfume.

'And that's the surprise for you,' said Emilie, extending her Christmas gift.

It was an LP of Neil Diamond's hit songs, including our favourites 'Play Me' and 'Sweet Caroline.'

'It's just what I needed. Thanks a lot,' I said.

The restaurant was to serve a five-course meal that evening with a variety of wines to choose from and Champagne to herald the New Year. It was around ten. People had downed sizeable quantities of wine and the atmosphere had livened up. Several couples were dancing in dim light.

'Do you like dancing?' Emilie asked.

'I can sort of jump around.'

'Then let's see you jump around.' Emilie laughed.

The next instant we were on the dance floor. Emilie could dance much better than me. We had gone through several songs but were in no mood to stop. Top hits were being played one after the other. And then came 'Play Me'. The song sent us into a trance and we stood still, clinging to each other. We came out of our ecstasy only when the song ended.

'We need some more food and wine,' Emilie said and we moved back to the table for dessert.

'A friend told me that Champs Elysees is the best place to welcome the New Year. Shall we go there a little before twelve?' I asked.

'Yes, it's a superb ambiance, but it's so cold outside,' Emilie was reluctant to leave the cozy restaurant.

'This is my only opportunity to see the New Year festivities at Champs Elysees. I'll not be here next year.'

'Why won't you be here next year?'

'I told you I am here just for a year and should go back around August.'

'You can't leave so fast,' Emilie complained.

'Well, I am not leaving tomorrow. I am here for at least eight months. So let's not worry about that. It's just that I am keen to see the merry making at the Champs Elysees,' I said.

'Let's go if it makes you happy. After all, we won't be alone in the cold,' Emilie said.

We pulled up along a street off the Champs Elysees about half an hour before twelve. A few drinks of cognac would help us fight the cold, Emilie suggested. So we walked into a nearby pub to brace ourselves for the cold outside.

It was a few minutes to twelve as we walked up to Arc de Triomphe. Thousands of revellers were converging on the Etoile with bottles of wine and Champagne in hand. The biting cold appeared to make no difference to their high spirits. Decorative lights all along Avenue de Champs Elysees added a colourful liveliness to the celebrations. At the stroke of midnight, a wave of joy swept through the crowd. People were yelling 'Bonne Annee' all around. I gave Emilie a tight hug and a kiss. The next moment we were swamped by a sea of unknown well-wishers, all hugging and kissing each other to convey greetings for the coming year.

The warmth of cognac gradually started wearing thin. I was not used to severe cold. Emilie sensed my predicament and said we should leave immediately. The crowd had also started melting away slowly.

By the time we reached Emilie's apartment block, I was in a terrible shape. The heating in the car had been completely ineffective.

'Why don't you come up for a cognac or coffee?' Emilie asked.

'A coffee would be lovely.' I grabbed the offer.

Emilie lived in a small, neatly kept one-room apartment. There was a mattress on the carpeted floor in one corner, a round dining table with four chairs on the other side, a small kitchen and a toilet. Emilie went to the kitchen to make coffee and I collapsed on the mattress. There were beautiful paintings on the walls. A rack close to the mattress contained a whole lot of books, mainly on French painters and scientific subjects, and a collection of music – LPs and cassettes.

'Café, Monsieur,' Emilie announced in a loud voice as she came carrying two cups of coffee.

'I was admiring your paintings. Did you buy them?' I asked.

'I painted these myself in the impressionist style. These are not much to look at but I shall take you one day to see the paintings of some great impressionist masters,' Emilie said.

'I find these adorable,' I said.

'I am glad someone likes them.'

'You also have a large collection of books and music,' I said.

'Well, I have been buying these from time to time because of my interest in painting and because the ever expanding scientific knowledge fascinates me. I hope our research team comes up with some major success this year. That would be absolutely great.'

'Is that a New Year resolve?' I asked.

'Sort of.'

'Let me wish you and your team all the best,' I said.

'And what is your New Year resolve?' Emilie asked.

'I wish to spend lots and lots of time with you.'

Emilie laughed and asked, 'Would you like to listen to some music?'

'I would love to.'

The choice fell upon our common idol – Neil Diamond. The charming melody of 'Sweet Caroline' filled the air and we were once again in each other's embrace. When the song ended, Emilie looked up and said, 'You seem to be very tired. Your eyes are bloodshot.'

'Yes, I am very tired,' I said putting my head in her lap and sprawling myself on the mattress.

'I love your hair,' Emilie said, moving her fingers through them.

'Because they are like Giovanni's?'

'No, silly. Because they are yours.'

I looked into her large blue eyes.

'Your eyes contain a sea of affection,' I murmured.

'I didn't know they were big enough to contain a sea,' she laughed.

She kept twirling my hair. I shut my eyes.

'May I call you Emie?' I mumbled.

'Sure and may I call you Lali?'

'Certainly.'

'Emie.'

'Yes.'

'I love you.'

'I love you too.'

'I wish this moment gets frozen in time and never comes to an end.'

'I wish so too, Lali. But you must go home now and take some rest.'

'Why can't I stay here,' I protested.

'There is just one mattress.'

'It should be good enough for both of us.'

'Now don't be naughty.'

'My car may not start in this cold,' I tried an excuse.

'In that case, I shall walk you to your home if you feel insecure going alone on foot.' Emilie was ready with a repartee.

Reaching the door, I turned, took Emilie in my arms and said, 'I don't feel like leaving you.'

'If you don't leave me, how will you meet me again,' she said.

'Strange logic.' I said, 'But you are right. The moment I leave you, I shall start harbouring the hope of seeing you again. That would be a nice feeling to live with. You must promise that you will meet me again very soon.'

'Promise.'

The phone ring woke me up. It was still dark. The fluorescent hands of my bedside clock showed it was twelve. 'Who could be ringing me up at midnight?' – I asked myself. As my thinking cleared a little, I recalled that I had gone to bed last night around 3 am and this had to be twelve of the next day. A look at the shutter across the window confirmed my conclusion as I could see daylight filtering through chinks in the metal.

It was a trunk call from India.

'Hello, Lalit. This is Papa here. Wish you a very happy new year, son!'

'Thanks Papa. A very happy new year to all of you too!' My voice was groggy.

'Lalit, I hope I didn't wake you up. What time do you get up in the mornings?'

'No Papa, you didn't wake me up. I have been up since eight.' I told a lie.

My father was proud of being one of the earliest birds in the city. He was up around five in the morning. A long morning walk, a bath with unheated water around the year, his morning prayers, a frugal breakfast and he was all set to start his working day by seven thirty or so. He would drive straight to his factory that worked in three shifts round the clock. Eight, I thought, was as far as I could go with him.

'Good. It's always good to be up early in the morning. I hope you are keeping well,' my father was pleased with my answer.

'Yes, I am fit and fine, Papa.'

'And I hope you don't drink too much,' my father asked.

This was another tricky question. My parents and the only brother were teetotallers. They knew that I had started taking alcohol since my college days. My father would often reproach me for breaking the family tradition. He reminded me that both his father and grandfather had been teetotallers. I refused to believe that in the long genealogy of my family, everyone had shunned the joys of drinking. However, the knowledge of our ancestry being confined up to the grandparents of my parents, I was unable to enlist the example of a drinking ancestor in my favour. I was sure that a mention of the previous night's heavy drinking would invite a strong retribution and most likely an instant recall to India. So, very reluctantly I suppressed the truth once again.

'No, Papa. I hardly ever drink.'

'Well, I wonder if I am getting an honest answer.' My father had his doubts.

'How are all of you in India, Papa?' I asked.

'We are fine and miss you a lot. Why haven't you called on Dr Petit? I gave you his address when you left. In his new year card he says you haven't contacted him.'

Dr Petit was a French physician and an India lover. He had met my father through a common friend during one of his frequent visits to India. The two had become great pals.

In fact, it was Dr Petit who had put my father in touch with Remedes.

'I have had a terribly busy schedule all this while, Papa. But things are going to be light over the next week or two. I'll try to visit him the coming weekend,' I said.

'Don't just try. Visit him,' my father ordered. 'He lives in a town the name of which is spelt the same way as the word 'tours' in English.'

'Shall do so, Papa.'

'Here, talk to your mother.'

'Hello, Lalit. It's been ages since you left. I miss you each minute.'

'I miss all of you too, Mama.'

'I hope you get to eat good nourishing food there.'

My mother was quick to focus on her one point obsession in her letters and phone calls to me.

'Mama, I have told you umpteen times that I like French food and get to eat Indian food once in a while.'

'Listen, I don't know what kind of tasteless food you get there. But I am told you get good quality milk. So, have three to four glasses of milk a day and remember don't touch beef.'

My mother's statement, music to the ears of the dairy industry, would have outraged promoters of French gastronomy. However, there was no point in selling French cuisine to her on a long distance call. She would discover it herself one day whenever she accompanied my father on one of his business trips to France. So, I acquiesced in her instructions too.

I had a brief chat with Udai and his wife Shobha.

'Don't forget to take plenty of milk, little baby.' Udai pulled my leg.

I rolled up the window shutter. 1st of January was a glorious day, bright and sunny, but very cold. I had a strong urge to hear Emilie's voice and dialled her number.

'Allo, Oui.'

'Emie, a very happy new year once again.'

'Hey, Lali! I was going to call you, but thought I might wake you up. A very happy new year to you too.'

'What are you doing today?' I asked.

'I am off to Poitiers again later today.'

'Again?'

'Yes. There is a family get together at my mother's place tomorrow. She just called and insisted I go back.'

'How long will you be gone?'

'Not too long. I should be back the coming Sunday.'

'That reminds me, I have to visit a place called Tours the coming weekend to meet a friend of my father who lives there. Do you know where this town is?' I asked.

'It's in the Loire region, south of Paris and not too far off from Angers.'

'Well, I shall talk to this gentleman later today and if he agrees I shall visit him on Saturday.'

'Listen, Poitiers is the next major town after Tours on the auto route from Paris to Bordeaux. Why don't you come to Poitiers on Saturday evening and we can come back to Paris on Sunday. I shall book a *pension* for your overnight stay.'

'That's a terrific idea.'

'See you on Saturday.'

'I love you Emie.'

'I love you too, Lali.' Nothing is more pleasant than repeated expression of newfound love.

I called Dr Petit. He said he would be out on Saturday, but be back home on Sunday. So I decided to go to Poitiers on Saturday, doing some sightseeing on the way. I borrowed a Remedes car and took the auto route from Paris to Orleans. From there I took the national route along the river Loire to Tours. The French kings had come to this region initially to take refuge from the burdens of power in Paris. Later on the Loire country had gradually turned into a pleasure retreat for rulers and a centre for artistic development. Italian artists – Leonardo da Vinci, Domenico de Cortona, Benevento Cellini – were commissioned to design luxurious castles and dwellings. On my way, I stopped by to see the castle of Chambord, the largest in the Loire Valley. It was designed in 1519 by Domenico de Cortona as a hunting lodge for the French King Francois I. Some say that da Vinci also played a role in its designing. Eventually, this lodge ended up having 84 staircases, 440 rooms and a chimney for every day of the year! No wonder it took several years and nearly two thousand workers to build. Its best known feature is the double helix staircase which has two separate spirals, leading to the roof, that entwine but never touch each other. The royal court used to gather on the roof to watch tournaments and the return of hunting parties.

It was past six and pitch dark when I reached the house of Emilie's mother. I rang the doorbell. A middle-aged lady opened the door. This was my first meeting with Mme Martin. She was impeccably dressed with a thick layer of make up on her face.

'Bonjour, Madame,' I greeted her.

'Bonjour,' she replied in a frosty tone.

'Mama, this is Lalit.' Emilie came running from inside to take charge of things.

'I see.' Madame Martin was curt. I was to learn later that this was her normal demeanour, accentuated by the misgivings she harboured about my relationship with her daughter.

'Why don't you step in?' Emilie asked.

She led me to the sitting room.

Uneasy silence prevailed for some time until Emilie broke it, 'Hope you had a pleasant journey.'

'Yes, it was enjoyable. I visited the castle of Chambord on the way.'

'Isn't it superb?' Emile said.

'It's magnificent and colossal,' I said.

There was again uneasy silence for a few seconds. Emilie gave an oblique fleeting glance to her mother, hoping she would say something. Mme Martin kept quiet. 'You must be feeling very cold. Let me make you some coffee,' Emile pushed off to the kitchen even before I could say whether I wanted a coffee. She was obviously uncomfortable with the situation.

I suddenly found myself alone in the awkward company of Mme Martin. Emilie, I noticed, had inherited her mother's features and hair. Mme Martin must have been a very pretty woman in her younger days. Later on, I thanked my stars on many occasions that Mme Martin had bequeathed only her looks and not her temperament to Emilie.

Mme Martin stared at me a few times as if to size me up. Finally, she asked me what I did for a living. I understood her question, but failed miserably as I tried to answer it in French. As I fumbled for words, Mme Martin's patience gave way and she too left for the kitchen saying a terse 'Excusez Moi'.

I looked around the living room. There was a picture of a middle-aged man and yet another one of a boy alongside it. There were a few paintings in the impressionist style, probably made by Emilie and some African artifacts.

Emilie and Mme Martin came back with coffee in a little while. We sipped it in silence until Emilie said, 'My father was a great admirer of India and her ancient civilisation.'

The mention of Monsieur Martin seemed to arouse Mme Martin's interest in the conversation.

'When we were in Paris many years ago, we used to see films by a famous Indian director once in a while. He was very good at portraying human feelings and the realities of life.'

Mme Martin finally spoke up. Emilie was visibly relieved and offered to be our interpreter.

'Do you remember his name?' I asked Mme Martin.

'No, I don't, but he was from Bengal.'

'You must be talking of Satyajit Ray.'

'That indeed was the name. Once my husband and I also attended a concert of Indian music. It was a string instrument, I think – Sitar.' She uttered the word Sitar with some difficulty.

'Have you been to India?' I asked.

'No, my husband had a keen desire to visit your country, but he could not fulfil it,' Mme Martin said, looking at the picture on the corner table with moist eyes. So that was the picture of Emilie's father.

'I hope you visit India sometime,' I said.

In response, Mme Martin said something that Emilie was reluctant to interpret. I could make out that she had said something about poverty and misery in India.

'Tell me what she says. You won't be a sincere interpreter if you hide anything,' I said with a smile.

Mme Martin, Emilie said, had heard a great deal about hunger, poverty and misery in India and was reluctant to see it with her own eyes. She felt she would find it emotionally very disturbing. Besides, she was not travelling very much in any case because of her poor health. Emilie added that Mma Martin was contributing to a charity for destitute children in India and wished she could do more. She apologised that her mother was bringing up such matters.

'You don't have to apologise. I have come across the same image of India amongst other friends here. An admiration for our rich past and a concern for the widespread poverty and related problems. We cannot wish our problems away and are trying to deal with them as best as we can,' I put up a brave front.

Emilie interpreted what I had said.

In response, Mme Martin again said something that Emile did not wish to interpret.

'Mama, must you say all this?' I could understand her say to Mme Martin in an irritated tone. When I insisted that Emilie tell me what Mme Martin had said, she put me off by saying that her mother had commented on a family matter. I knew that was not the case, but decided against pressing a visibly embarrassed Emilie for an honest answer.

'You have beautiful paintings and a superb collection of African artifacts,' I told Mme Martin to change the topic. She did not respond and sat with a sullen face. Emilie said they had lived in Africa for some years and had acquired the artifacts at that time. With Mme Martin refusing to talk, our conversation had reached a virtual dead end and could clearly not proceed any further. Mme Martin excused herself saying she was not too well and needed rest. Emilie said she would prepare something for dinner. She brought a portable TV from inside and put on a lively musical programme for me.

'You will have a surprise for dinner and it won't be long,' she said and disappeared into the kitchen.

It was indeed fast work as she appeared within a short while with a pan containing melted cheese. She lit a flame, put the pan on it and brought a basket full of baguette bread broken into small pieces.

'Voila! Our meal is ready. Do you know what it is?'

'Isn't it fondue?' I asked.

'O, no! It's not after all a surprise for you,' Emilie was disappointed.

'I know just the name. I have seen it being served in restaurants on a few occasions and a friend told me it's called fondue. But I have never tasted it.'

'Good, then try it. Take a piece of bread with that long stemmed fork, twirl it in cheese and see if you like it. I shall in the meanwhile open a bottle of white wine,' Emilie said.

'Hmmm! This is delicious,' I said.

'It's a great dish for winter, especially when served with a good white wine,' Emilie said, pouring some wine in my glass.

'Isn't your mother going to join us?' I asked.

'She says she needs rest.'

'Hope it's nothing serious.'

'No, she is just a little tired.'

I knew it was not true. In fact, Mme Martin was done with me for the evening.

'Does your mother live here alone?' I asked.

'Yes, since the passing away of my father. She works in a bank. My father was an engineer working with a construction company of Marseille on projects in Africa. He died in an air crash six years ago while on his way back from Abidjan.'

'I am sorry to know that. Is that your father's photo?'

'Yes. And that one next to his is that of my brother. He died four years ago. Had a massive brain haemorrhage and was gone within twelve hours,' Emilie said, wiping the tears that had trickled down her cheeks.

'I am awfully sorry. I shouldn't have brought up this painful topic.'

'You don't have to feel bad. It's just that my anger boils over every now and then at the thought of the tragedies that my family has suffered.'

'Such tragedies are God's will and we humans can do nothing about them. We must learn to accept them,' I tried to console Emilie.

'If indeed there is God to will such things, He has been very cruel to us.'

'I am sure He has his reasons. It's just that we cannot explain them.'

'What reason could He have to take away my brother? He was just fifteen.' Emilie was sobbing. I held her hand.

'Thanks for making this delicious fondue,' I said to change the topic when Emilie calmed down.

'I am glad you liked it,' she said with a faint smile.

'I simply loved it. Will you please make it more often for me in Paris?'

'Sure.'

We wound up the dinner with some hot apple pie and coffee.

'I booked a *pension* for you down this street,' Emilie said.

'Why can't we stay together at the *pension*?' I pleaded.

'My mother will not be amused if I leave her and stay with you. You must have patience.'

'How long?'

'A bit longer.'

'My patience is wearing thin. If I am found dead at the *pension* tomorrow morning, you should know that I died of impatience.'

'What is the hurry to die? Exercise some patience before you die of impatience.' Emilie burst out laughing.

'Youuuuuuuuuuu..........' I was not amused.

The *pension* was barely two hundred metres down the road. We decided to meet at nine thirty the next morning and do some sightseeing in Poitiers before leaving for Tours.

Poitiers used to be the capital of the Poitou region of France – a region of sunflower fields. A city of barely eighty thousand inhabitants – many of them students at the famous local university – it is sometimes called the 'smallest of the big cities' of France. It is located on a hilltop with two rivers – Clain and Boivre – running around it. We walked around the streets of Poitiers, starting with the market square of Place Charles de Gaulle. We saw the beautiful Romanesque church – Notre Dame la Grande – that dates from the 13th century. We finally wound up for lunch in a café in the main city square – Place Marechal Leclerc.

'Did you like Poitiers?' Emilie asked.

'It's lovely. But I sorely missed you last night.'

'I only asked you to say if you liked Poitiers,' Emilie said, emphasising each of the last four words.

'I told you the city is lovely but I sorely missed you last night. I couldn't bear the thought that you were only two hundred metres away from me and yet had left me alone.'

'Patience, my dear Lali, patience,' Emilie said in a teasing tone.

'I am going to lose it one of these days.'

'You must never act against the wishes of a woman. That's what the folktale of this region concerning fairy Melusine tells us.'

'Fairy what?'

'Melusine. Let me tell you her story.'

Emilie proceeded to narrate it.

Melusine was the daughter of the fairy Pressyne and King Elynas of Albany. She became the fairy queen of the forest of Colombier in the Poitou region. One day, while guarding a sacred fountain, she met a young man, Raymond of Poitiers. They talked the whole night and were betrothed by the morning, but with a condition. Raymond was asked to promise that he would never see Melusine on a Saturday. He agreed and they got married. The legend has it that she built many castles, churches, towers and towns in the region – each one in one night. She is said to have made the fortress of Lusignan very quickly by magic. Melusine and Raymond had ten children, but each one of them had a flaw. For example, one of them had a lion's foot jutting out of his cheek, another one had only one eye and yet another one had a great tooth. One day Raymond grew very suspicious of the Saturday activities of his wife. He saw her bathing on a Saturday through a keyhole. He found that she had the body of a serpent waist down. He said nothing until their son with a great tooth killed many monks at a monastery. Raymond accused Melusine of contaminating his children with her serpent blood and thus gave away his having seen her on a Saturday. Melusine immediately turned into a serpent and flew away. She would come at night to visit her children. Raymond was never happy again. Melusine appeared at the castle, wailing, each time a count of Lusignan was dying or one was to be born. It was believed that her descendants would rule the world till its end.

'She imposed a tough condition on poor Raymond. Love means complete trust and she should have told him what she did on Saturdays,' I said when Emilie was done with the tale.

'If love means complete trust, Raymond shouldn't have harboured suspicions about his wife's Saturday activities.'

'Listen; now don't try to scare me with your Melusine story. First of all, I am absolutely sure that you are not a serpent waist downwards. And I also know that if we have children, they will have normal teeth, two eyes and none of them will have a lion's foot jutting out of his cheek. So don't be surprised if I act against your wishes out of exasperation.'

'How can you be so sure about me? You may well end up with a poisonous bite.'

'I would much rather die of such a bite than live this life of fortitude and chastity.'

Emilie laughed.

It was around one thirty when we hit the road to Tours. As we moved away from Poitiers, my mind went back to Mme Martin.

'What does Mme Martin think of our relationship?' I asked.

'I don't care about what she thinks.'

'You can't do that. You are her only child.'

'I have always understood my responsibilities as her only child. But she had no business talking unpleasant stuff in front of you.'

'I told you I didn't mind what she said. I know well my country's problems and one could not reproach her for referring to them. However, she seems to have an exaggerated notion of those problems.'

'Precisely, India is not all poverty and misery.'

'You mustn't make too much of her ignorance.'

'I wouldn't have but for the fact that she was very nasty towards the end. You know what she said?'

'What?'

'She said her generation had seen a lot of despair during the Second World War. But having lived in peace and prosperity thereafter, even people of her generation would find it difficult to support emotionally the desperate situation in countries like India. She then went on to say that it would be all the more difficult for a person of my generation, who had seen only prosperity, to live in a country like India.'

Emilie had blurted out in a fit of rage what she had been reluctant to interpret the previous evening. I made no comment.

'I think she stretched it too far,' Emilie was livid.

'Let's not worry too much about it. I am sure she will have a better understanding of our relationship with passage of time.'

'Let's hope so.' Emilie's tone was a little calmer than before. She fell silent.

'Why did Mme Martin talk of someone of Emilie's generation having to live in India?' I asked myself. After all neither

Emilie nor I had raised that possibility. And yet, my growing relationship with Emilie had the seeds of that outcome. There was some point to what Mme Martin had said, even though she had spoken of a scenario which was still far-fetched and a mere possibility in future.

'Why are you bothered about such issues? You still have sufficient time in France to sort them out,' something within me said. I put my mind at ease. Emilie had already gotten over her anger and dozed off. I put my hand on hers and pressed it gently. She stirred out of her sleep, smiled, patted my head and again dozed off.

Dr Petit lived on the outskirts of Tours. He and his wife extended us a very warm welcome. He recounted his association with India and how he had come into contact with my father. He thought my apprenticeship with Remedes would give me a solid base in pharmaceuticals business. We were treated to hot coffee and exquisite French patisserie. Dr Petit complimented Emilie on her good English and said, 'Now you must make sure that this young man learn good French.'

'I attend French classes at L'Institut Catholique,' I said.

'That's all very well, but I can tell you that there is no better way of learning a language than having a girlfriend who speaks that language,' Dr Petit laughed.

We left for Paris, promising to remain in touch with him.

We had not gone very far when the temperature of the cooling fluid in the car engine rose unusually. I switched off the engine. The fluid level was all right and there was nothing apparently wrong. We restarted when the engine had cooled down, but the trouble resurfaced. It was with great difficulty that we reached a petrol pump in the next small town. The proprietor was winding up and it took some pleading to persuade him to have a look at the engine. He said it was a defect in the radiator and could be fixed only the next morning. He became prickly when we asked him if something could be done right away.

'Look here Monsieur, if you are in that much of a hurry, please take your car away. But if you can wait till tomorrow, you can leave it here and we will look at it in the morning.'

Sensing trouble, we thanked the man profusely for his agreeing to let us leave the car at his station and walked into a nearby bistro. It was around midnight, after a series of drinks; we reached a lodge suggested by the bistro owner. The proprietor of the lodge looked visibly upset at being woken up at that hour. However, seeing prospective clients, he kept his cool and showed us our room on the first floor. It was in a dilapidated state with wallpaper peeling off at many places. The carpet was worn out. The small toilet in one corner was not well-cleaned.

'What do you say?' I asked in a whisper.

'You can't expect five-star luxury in this town,' Emilie said. 'Beggars can't be choosers.'

I gave a nod. The proprietor wished us 'Bonne Nuit' in a sleepy voice and looked relieved to be going back to his interrupted sleep.

'Let's change,' said Emile, disappearing into the toilet.

I was already in my nightclothes and in bed when she emerged from the toilet in a nightie. I could not help staring at her.

'Don't ogle me like that,' she admonished and got into her bed.

'I can't help it. You look ravishing.'

'We must get some sleep now, Lali.'

'I am not sleepy.'

'Put naughty thoughts out of your mind and you will sleep well.'

I could hear Emilie tossing and turning for the next few minutes. The room was overheated. I tried to reduce the heating, but the control knob of the radiator was jammed. Emilie suggested we leave the only window of the room slightly open. As soon as I opened the window a bit, the strong breeze outside flung it wide open and I had to struggle to shut it again. We contemplated contacting the proprietor to get the heating reduced, but did not have the courage to wake him up again. He seemed to have made up for flaws in the room by giving us an excessive dose of heating!

Emilie eventually gave up trying to sleep and picked up a magazine to read. It was a three-months-old issue of *Paris-Match*, probably left in the room by a client. Having nothing else to do, I decided to make a serious attempt to sleep, took off my nightshirt and dozed off in a few minutes. Not that I did not have other ideas, but Emilie had shown no interest in anything other than reading.

I woke up perspiring. Emilie was reclining on her side with her back towards me. She had taken off her nightie and had pulled the bedsheet up to the waist. She was still reading and did not realise that I was awake. She had an elbow on the pillow, with an upright forearm and hand supporting her head to enable her read. Her auburn hair lay scattered on the pillow. Looking at her back, for a moment I had an illusion of having in front of me a perfectly sculpted figure of a Greek goddess – the kind I had seen in museums. It was only the gentle breathing movement of her waist that told me it was my Emie. I had a strong urge to take her in my arms but resisted it.

I shut my eyes in a futile attempt to sleep. In a few minutes, I heard Emilie take a turn. I opened my eyes. She was still reclining on her side, this time facing me, with the magazine in front of her. She gave me a momentary glance and then lowered her eyes to the magazine. Her fingers flipped through it quickly from cover to cover in a nervous movement, without her pausing to look at any particular page. My gaze remained fixed on her. She repeated the same sequence, as if unconsciously, three or four times. I moved over to her bed and showered her with a thousand little kisses.

We were soon locked in a tight embrace – an embrace of infinite passion.

'Lali.'

'Yes, my love.'

'Where are you taking me?'

'Just follow me, ma chere Emie.'

And then somewhere along the way we got completely lost in each other. The world around us vanished. The entire existence had boiled down to the two of us – Emilie and Lalit. Lalit and Emilie. Nothing else existed. Nothing else mattered. A few more moments and even Emilie and Lalit vanished. All that remained was an immense sea of love. Nothing else existed. Nothing else mattered. Our journey finally ended in a moment of timelessness, a state of ecstasy – pure and simple.

The vanished world reappeared gradually with Emilie and Lalit in it – lying side by side, utterly sated.

They say time flies and it flies even faster when one's life is full of joy. I found my training with Remedes fascinating. That took care of the working week. And most of my evenings and weekends were spent in Emilie's amorous company. Our love had grown with each passing day. This woman, I had not even known only a few months ago, had become the core and purpose of my life. So long as she was mine, nothing else mattered. We found interminable charm, affection and happiness in each other.

It was a Saturday in the first week of March – around ten in the morning. The phone rang. Emilie was to visit her mother that weekend. Sunil and I had planned a binge in the evening. Must be Sunil calling to confirm the evening plans, I thought.

'Allo, Lali.' It was Emilie.

'Where are you calling from, my love? I thought you would be on a train to Poitiers at this time.'

'No, I am in Paris. My mother had to leave all of a sudden for Marseille early in the morning to attend the funeral of her cousin. The poor lady had been ailing for quite some time. So I cancelled my visit to Poitiers.'

'I am awfully sorry.'

'What are your plans for the day?'

'Nothing in particular. I was preparing to do my laundry during the day. It's such a drag every two weeks, you know. Sunil and I had planned an outing in the evening. But now that you are here, why don't we meet. We can have lunch together.'

'Look I don't want to spoil your plans.'

'Now don't be so formal Emilie. You sound so low. It's normal with this news of your aunt. I wouldn't like you to be alone today.'

'You are such a sweetheart, Lali.'

'I have an idea. You have been speaking of this museum of impressionist paintings. Let's visit it today and then go for lunch somewhere.'

'You mean the Marmottan museum?'

'The one that has the famous impressionist paintings by Monet. You remember you showed me their reproductions in a book the other day.'

'Yes, they are in Marmottan museum in the 16th district.'

We met at the museum that, Emilie explained, contained the largest collection of paintings by Claude Monet. The impressionist style, she said, focused on the general impression produced by a scene and Monet had produced masterpieces by recording the transient effects of light and colour. Besides the famous painting – Impression Sunrise – that gave impressionism its name, the museum also had some delightful paintings of water lilies, irises, rose arbours and Japanese bridges from Monet's garden. Monet had captured the impression of each scene at various times of the day with changing light and its interplay with colours. The garden, Emilie said, could be seen even today in a place called Giverny, some seventy kilometres from Paris, where Monet lived for over forty years till his death in 1926. That's where he laid his jardin d'eau or water garden. Giverny would open to visitors April onwards and Emilie said we could go there sometime.

Our next stop was Quartier Latin or the Latin Quarter of Paris. The famous Sorbonne University was first established here, even though it is now spread all over the city. They say Latin was spoken here in the past. Hence its name. It had attracted me ever so often for its vivacity. The city of Paris had its origins in the nearby Ile de la Cite, an island in the river Seine. The Romans conquered the Parisii tribe in 52 BC and established themselves on Ile de la Cite. They slowly extended their settlements along the Left Bank in the modern day Quartier Latin. They built a Forum, an amphitheatre, an aqueduct, thermal baths and roads in the area. Cluny Museum of medieval art is located on the site of an ancient thermal bath. Le Pantheon, commemorating the dead heroes of France, is located on top of the Mount Sainte Genevieve, named after a brave girl who is believed to have united the Parisians during the barbarian raids. Eating in Quartier Latin had been one of our favourite pastimes – especially in its Greek and Lebanese restaurants. That day we went to a Greek restaurant on Rue de la Harpe, a cobblestone street near the famous Boulevard Saint-Germain. I took a Donner kebab. Emilie ate very little saying she had had heavy breakfast. She was still visibly upset and not her usual self. I hoped I had been of some help to her in overcoming the grief of her aunt's death.

Once we finished our meal, I proposed to walk down to the famous Notre Dame church on Ile de la Cite. I was keen that in the frame of mind in which she was, Emilie should stay outside her home for as long as possible. Besides, a visit to the church might help. I had been to Notre Dame twice on my own in the past, but it was the first time that I was visiting it with Emilie. She explained to me its history. I noticed that she did not pause to pray or light a candle. She stayed there much like a tourist. I found her behaviour odd.

We took the metro back to Emilie's studio. She went to the kitchen to make some coffee. I followed her.

'Look Emilie, I know you too well to realise that you are awfully upset about something. It's perhaps the death of your aunt. You must talk to me about whatever is bothering you. That may alleviate your pain. Don't keep it within yourself.'

Emile burst out crying. I took her in my arms. When she was able to subdue her emotions a bit, she said, 'This is the day my brother died four years ago.'

'I can understand your pain. One has no option but to endure it. You should look to the future and pray to God for the best. That's the only way you can bear the loss of a loved one.'

'Do you think prayer helps? I don't think so,' Emilie said.

'Beg your pardon?' Emilie's question left me perplexed.

'My mother has always been religious minded. While my brother struggled for his life, she constantly prayed for his recovery. But that didn't save him.' Emilie burst out crying.

'You have indeed been through very tragic circumstances. But you must maintain a positive attitude in life and mustn't lose faith in God.'

'If there is indeed a God, I can't help questioning His justice. My brother had his entire life ahead of him and one day it was brutally cut short. It all leaves me so angry.' Emile was sobbing.

'Look I have an idea. Let's listen to your music collection and have dinner together. I haven't had fondue for a long time. Will you make it for me?' I changed the topic.

'Sure,' she said wiping her tears.

I called Sunil to cancel our rendezvous. He delivered a long lecture on the virtues of not giving in completely to the influence of a woman. I said I would listen to his homily some other day.

Emile and I listened to music, had fondue, and as time went by, her mood improved. We talked late into the evening and made love.

I had done eleven months of training with Remedes. It was the 15th of August. It being the vacation period, most of the Parisians had left for other tourist spots and Paris itself appeared to be under invasion from a large number of foreign tourists. The Remedes bosses had kept all their production lines functional, though far below the normal capacity. This meant that there was no break in my training. I had been told that I had no time to lose and must use each day to learn more about the Remedes production processes. I had with great difficulty managed a week's visit to Brussels with Emilie.

I reached the factory two hours late after attending the Independence Day flag hoisting at the Indian Embassy. The unit in-charge, who had permitted me to come late, felicitated me on India's Independence Day and said that he was glad Indians had chased away the English. I found the comment amusing, coming as it did from the citizen of a country that had itself been a colonial power. I found such comments about the English, made by my French friends, very interesting. Here were two countries that, because of their geographic proximity and shared history, had a lot in common. And yet, their shared history had also bequeathed them a love-hate relationship and a spirit of competition. It had amused me no end to learn in the course of my French lessons that unauthorised absence from work, that the English had taught us to call 'French leave', was described by the French as 'Filer a l'anglaise', which meant 'to run away like the English'! I thanked the unit in-charge for his felicitations and invited him to have lunch with me at an Indian restaurant. The invitation was readily accepted. As I turned to go to my slot in the production line, he said, 'Ah, yes, Gaston Lafond wishes to see you this morning. They called from Boulogne. We could perhaps meet directly at the Indian restaurant once you are through with him.'

Lafond was the marketing manager of Remedes. I hated the thought of seeing him. He was a morose and grumpy old man, disliked by most in the company. Even though I had worked mostly with the production people, Lafond being the liaison man between Remedes and my father's company was formally in-charge of my training. I had met him briefly in the beginning and thereafter on a few occasions. He was known to shout at people at the slightest pretext and I hoped I wasn't in for a shock treatment. It was in an anxious frame of mind that I left for Boulogne.

Lafond was castigating someone on the phone when I entered his office. I stood, awaiting his permission to sit down, as he finished with the phone call and thumbed through a file. It was after an interminable tense period of a few minutes that he looked up.

'Bonjour, Monsieur,' I promptly greeted him.

'Bonjour. Why don't you sit down?' His tone was curt.

I gingerly pulled a chair and sat down. Lafond went back to his work and it was after another interminable period of five minutes that he looked at me again.

'How long have you been with us?' he asked.

'About eleven months, Monsieur.'

'I have been getting reports on your training from the production side. I am glad you have done well.'

I was relieved to hear that he was not unhappy with my work. I also noticed that his satisfaction with my work, expressed in words, failed to reveal itself in his facial expression which remained as glum as ever.

'Merci, Monsieur,' I muttered.

'Which unit are you in now?'

'The antibiotics section, Monsieur.'

'You should get ready to go back home by mid-September. You could stay on in the antibiotics section for another two weeks. You must then spend two weeks with our accounts people. That's an area in which we have problems with your side, perhaps because your people are not familiar with our accounting requirements. I would like you to take your accounts training seriously.'

I remained quiet. My mind had drifted elsewhere. I had all along known that I would return to India in September. But now Lafond had announced my impending departure formally. What was to happen to my relationship with Emilie? The question had now assumed urgency and had to be faced squarely. Lafond asked me if I needed any clarifications. My mind took a few seconds to register his query.

'No, Monsieur.' I thanked him and came out of his office.

As I walked absentmindedly towards the exit door, someone tapped me on the shoulder.

'Bonjour, Lalit. Comment ca va?'

I turned. It was Raymond Dufour, the production manager of Remedes. A man in his late fifties, he was a highly gregarious and popular person. A bachelor, he would often say that there was much more fun in remaining an eligible bachelor than in getting married. The number of women who fell for him left no one in doubt that he was indeed an eligible bachelor despite his age. He was about the same seniority as Lafond, but very informal and kind to his subordinates.

'Ca va bien, Monsieur,' I was pleased to see Dufour after my tense meeting with Lafond. 'You seem to have spent some days in bright sunshine.' The suntan was clear on his face.

'Well, I spent three marvellous weeks in Greece. The sun, the sea, great food and above all pretty women of various nationalities. What more could one ask for, mon cher Lalit,' he said with a hearty laugh.

'I am glad you enjoyed your vacation, Monsieur.'

'Tell me about yourself. How is your training proceeding?'

'Very well, Monsieur. In fact I'll complete it next month and leave for India.'

'What a pity. You train someone into an outstanding chemist, only to lose him. I wish I could retain you in my production line. Anyway you will do us some good in being with your father's factory. Drop by sometime.'

'Certainly, Monsieur.'

Before I left the Remedes headquarters, I called Emilie.

'Emie, could you come by to my place this evening?'

'Anything special?'

'No, I just want to have a little chat with you.'

'About what?'

'Let's meet and talk.'

Emilie arrived in the evening. I had spent an extremely restless day with the exception of a few light moments during my lunch with my unit in-charge.

'Mon Dieu! It's so hot,' Emilie said flinging herself on the nearest chair. 'I am exhausted.'

'Shall I fix you a drink?'

'Yes please. A big glass of any soft drink with lots of ice.'

'What's it you wanted to talk to me about?' she asked as I emerged from the kitchen with her drink.

'Nothing important. We could talk about it a little later,' I said.

I had involuntarily uttered these words that sounded so hollow to my own ears. What a ridiculous statement to make, I thought. Nothing was more important to me at that stage than the subject I wanted to discuss with Emilie. Our relationship had crossed many stages without our ever pausing to think what direction it would eventually take. This question had cropped up in my mind several times, but I had brushed it aside, telling myself each time that there was plenty of time to sort it out. Now time had practically run out. I was sure Emilie too knew what I wanted to talk about and yet, ostrich like, both of us were keen to postpone the difficult issue, if only for a few hours.

Instead of persisting with her question, Emilie grabbed the first opportunity to change the topic as her eyes fell on my collection of books.

'Hullo! What do I see here? Some new books.' She had seen a collection of Victor Hugo's romantic plays and two volumes of De Gaulle's memoirs that I had acquired a few days earlier.

'I bought these from a bouquiniste on the Left Bank.' My reference was to a second-hand bookseller on the Left Bank of the Seine River in the Latin Quarter. There was a delightful collection of old books at the bookstalls there.

'I wonder if your French is good enough to read these.'

'That's precisely the problem. I tried reading Victor Hugo, but had to look up the dictionary every now and then. That spoils the fun of reading. Now that gives me an idea. Why don't you read me one of the plays and explain difficult portions in English?'

'That won't be easy either.'

'Let's try it out.'

'All right let's try it out,' Emilie said picking up the book. Thumbing through it, she picked up one of the plays – *La Esmeralda* – that she said was her favourite. It is the story of an Egyptian dancer – La Esmeralda – in a king's court, who falls in love with a captain in his army – Phoebus de Chateaupers.

I pulled up a chair alongside Emilie's as she read the play. We came upon a stanza that I liked immensely and remember till today. It is addressed by Phoebus to La Esmeralda and goes something like this: Fee ou femme,Sois ma dame!Car mon ame,Nuit et jour,Te desire,Te respire,Et t'admire,Mon amour!

Emilie fell silent after reading this stanza.

'Why are you keeping quiet? Let's have the translation,' I said.

'Why must you insist on it? It's fairly simple and I am sure you understand it.'

'Not fully.'

'All right if you must have the exact translation, this is how I think it should go: O, fairy-like woman, Be my wife! Because my soul, Day and night, Longs for you, With each breath, And adores you, My love!'

Silence ensued. Emilie's gaze was fixed on the book.

'Emie.'

There was no answer.

'Emie. I am talking to you.'

There was still no answer.

'Emie, are you listening to me?'

'Yes, I am.'

'Let me tell you that I feel for you the same way as Phoebus for La Esmeralda. I wish I could express my feelings even more forcefully. Will you marry me?'

There was again no response and Emilie turned her face away from me.

'I am waiting for your answer, my love.'

She kept quiet. I turned her face gently towards me. Her eyes were brimming with tears.

'Emie, you got to be frank with me,' I said.

'Lali, you know how much I love you. I can't bear the thought of staying without you. But I have a responsibility towards my mother. She has no one else to look after her. I must talk to her before I answer you.'

'Of course, you must talk to your mother. I don't want an answer today itself,' I reassured Emilie. 'I would be leaving for India by mid-September.'

'I am going to Poitiers the coming weekend. That should give me an opportunity to talk to my mother.'

'Has she ever given you an indication of what she thinks of our relationship?'

'Well, she has been hinting every now and then – you heard it once yourself – that it would be impossible for me to adjust to life in India. I don't care about that. Your love should help me get over whatever difficulties I may face. But I don't want to give my mother the feeling of being deserted. I must persuade her to let me go.'

'I wish I could stay on in France.'

'No, Lali. Your family needs you. Your father needs you to help him with his business.'

There was nothing more to be said. We resumed our reading of 'La Esmeralda'. The play ended on a tragic note with Phoebus getting killed by a priest whose advances had been spurned by La Esmeralda. It left me depressed.

Emilie lay by my side through the night, trying to sleep. She tossed and turned most of the time. So did I.

Emilie left early next morning. She was to be at work at eight. The sleeplessness of the previous night had left my head throbbing with pain. In the midst of that restless night, the idea of staying on in France had gripped me. Its impracticality and negative consequences paled into insignificance in front of my intense desire not to leave Emilie.

'I wish I could retain you in my production unit,' Raymond Dufour's words rang in my ears. Was it a mere wish or would he proceed to implement his idea on my request? The answer was clear, but I refused to accept the reality and lose the only silver lining in an otherwise bleak scenario.

Dufour would be in office by nine. Nine thirty would be a good time to call him. I rang up my unit in-charge and took his permission to be late to work. I sat in front of the clock, watching its seconds hand tick away, giving me reassurance of movement of time. It was ages before its hour and minute hands completed their laborious journey to be in position for nine thirty.

The phone had barely started ringing when Dufour's secretary answered. Mme Masmejean was a good friend of mine. Her husband worked at Quai d'Orsay and had done a posting in the French Embassy in Delhi. They had invited me a few times to their home for a meal. She would often boast of her negotiating skills for she had driven several hard bargains with the shopkeepers at Janpath in Delhi. She was a kind and happy-go-lucky woman. However, today her voice sounded tense.

'Is that Mme Masmejean?' I asked.

'Oui.'

'Madame, this is Lalit here.'

'Yes, please go on. I am in a hurry.'

'Hope all is well.'

'No, all is not well. Raymond has bitten my nose off several times since he entered the office this morning.'

'Good Lord! That's so uncharacteristic of him.'

'Yes. It's some newly purchased machinery that broke down yesterday evening and the suppliers are not very helpful. The Managing Director is hopping mad and has driven Raymond crazy. Anyway, let me know quickly what I can do for you.'

'Could I talk to Monsieur Dufour?'

'Oh la la! It seems you didn't register what I just told you. Raymond is in no frame of mind to think of anything other than the faulty machinery at this moment.'

'Look, it's an urgent matter and I expect a little more sympathy from a good friend like you,' I persisted.

'Lalit, I never knew people could be so stubborn.' Mme Masmejean was understandably angry, but the clicking sound the very next moment told me that she had proceeded to put me through to Dufour.

'Allo, oui.' Dufour also sounded terribly hard-pressed for time.

'Lalit here, Monsieur. I would like to see you today for a few minutes.'

'Oh, no. Not today. Check with Masmejean if she can give you some time tomorrow.'

'Monsieur, it's something very urgent and important for me.'

'God! Why do all matters of life and death crop up the same day?'

'Monsieur, I wouldn't bother you if it were not urgent. I need only a few minutes.'

'All right, come after twelve. I may be able to see you close to lunch time.'

I was happy to get an appointment. The matter could have certainly waited for one more day but in my restless state of mind, I wanted to proceed as quickly as possible. At the same time I was also disappointed that Raymond had to be stressed on a day I was going to ask for a favour of him, which would take a lot in giving. I reached his office a little after twelve and gingerly opened the door to Masmejean's room. To my utter surprise, she looked very relaxed and welcomed me with a warm smile.

'Looks like the storm has blown over,' I said.

'Thank God it has. The suppliers came soon after your phone call and promised to get things fixed by tomorrow.'

I heaved a sigh of relief and said, 'Poor you! You had to suffer for no fault of yours this morning.'

'Well, that's the misfortune of us secretaries. We are at the receiving end, whatever the source of annoyance of the boss.'

Dufour called me in as soon as he was informed of my arrival. He too looked relaxed.

'Tell me Lalit, what brings you here.'

'Monsieur, you recall, you had expressed a wish to retain me in your production line when we met yesterday.'

'Yes, but ...'

'Monsieur, I desperately need to stay on here and hope to get your help.'

'But we will need you to run our production line in India and you must remember that Gaston will kill me if I ever suggest your continued stay here.'

'Monsieur, I told you that it's personally very important for me that I stay on here.'

Dufour peered at me and asked, 'Is it a woman?'

I nodded in affirmation.

'I never thought you would do something as foolish as that,' Dufour thundered. 'I hate to see vigorous young men like you pine away in starry-eyed pursuit of a woman as if the number of the female segment of the human species has dwindled to one. This life is too precious to waste on a single individual. Look around you. There is any number of them wherever you go. If you are at a loose end, go to Bois de Boulogne and you will find women to take care of your evening. But for God's sake, don't spend the best part of your life chasing one woman. Leave that to romantic literature,' he thumped his desk to emphasise the last two sentences.

The advice was typical of the man. He was known to have had many women in his life and I don't think was ever at a loose end, necessitating a visit to Bois de Boulogne. He had stirred a hornet's nest at a Remedes party when talking about the increasing incidence of divorce; he had said that man was not monogamous by nature. He elaborated his statement by saying that in older days, women would die during childbirth, giving the husband a chance to marry again. Now that better health care ensured longevity of women, the increasing number of divorces was a logical consequence. The women at the party were up in arms and had obliged Dufour to depart prematurely from the scene.

I knew that there was no point in countering his views that were a matter of conviction for him. I kept quiet hoping that his heart would melt at my plight. After all he was known to be a very helpful man.

'Who is this lady?' he asked after a few seconds' heavy silence.

'She is from Poitiers and works as a medical researcher here.'

'I pray to God to extricate you from this mess. However, let me see what I can do to help you through your current predicament. I shall be asking for your retention at the cost of unpleasantness with Gaston. But I don't mind taking a bit of flak for a good chap like you.'

Dufour's assurance of help came as a plank for a shipwrecked person. I thanked him profusely and came away.

I rang up Emilie in the evening to give her the news of my meeting with Dufour. She was annoyed that I was entertaining the thought of staying on in France, which would certainly be opposed by my family. She promised to persuade her mother to let her go with me and said she would let me know the outcome as soon as she came back from Poitiers.

Emilie, who had gone to Poitiers only for the weekend, had not returned even though it was Wednesday. Attempts by me to contact her had failed. Each time the phone was taken by Mme Martin who banged the receiver the moment she realised it was me. Emilie's demarche with her had obviously not produced the desired result, though I would have to wait till Emilie returned to find out what exactly had transpired. Dufour had also not called. He was a man of quick action and would certainly have acted on my request by then. Had he also encountered a dead end? The thought worried me.

'Lalit phone call for you from Boulogne,' my unit in-charge shouted from his cabin at the other end of the hall.

My heart leapt. Must be Dufour.

'Am I talking to Monsieur Lalit?' It was a lady's voice.

'Yes, this is Lalit.'

'This is Monsieur Lafond's secretary. He wishes to see you urgently. Would you please come to Boulogne right away?'

Lafond was the last person I wanted to see. The thought of meeting him made me nervous.

Lafond's secretary ushered me in.

'Tell the accountant to see me at four today. He has made a mess of this statement,' Lafond barked at his secretary, looking at her from above his half glasses and holding a paper in his hand.

The secretary nodded in confirmation of having heard his instructions, if a confirmation was at all required, Lafond's instructions having been conveyed in at least six times the requisite number of decibels. My heart sank. I wasn't expecting a pleasant encounter, but seeing Lafond's temper, it was going to be much worse than expected.

'I understand you are out to swindle Remedes,' he yelled without asking me to take a seat.

I knew I had asked for something unreasonable of the Remedes management, but I failed to see how it amounted to swindling. My blood boiled but I held myself back.

'I don't follow you, Monsieur,' I said as politely as I could under the circumstances.

'What you are trying to do is nothing short of swindling. We spend so much to train you to run our operations in India and you want to use that training to stay on in France. You can't do it so long as I am around.'

'But I have some good personal reasons for the request I have made.' I made a feeble attempt to remonstrate with him. 'Then the interests of Remedes and those of your father's business better take precedence over your own misguided interests.'

'Monsieur, if only you would let me explain...'

'I need no explanation. I won't let you get away with swindling of our company. You can try as hard as you can through that Casanova.' His reference was to Dufour.

'You ought to watch your words, Monsieur. I wonder if you know what "swindle" means,' the rage within me had finally overpowered my patience.

'Good Lord! Now these youngsters will improve our vocabulary! Now listen carefully. I warn you for the last time not to take advantage of what Remedes has done for you. I give you two days to confirm that you are going back. Failing that, I'll approach your father and take whatever steps are necessary to enforce our understanding about your training.' His face was scarlet.

Before I could say anything further, Lafond thundered, 'And I have no more time to waste. So do me the favour of leaving my office immediately.'

I turned to leave only to hear another scream behind me, 'Lastly, I must warn you. I have the backing of the Director General. So don't let Raymond fool you with false hopes.'

My feet turned, of their own accord, towards Dufour's office. I utilised the few seconds that it took me to reach his office to assess my situation. I cursed myself for having lost my temper towards the end of my meeting with Lafond. But then it was clear that regardless of my behaviour with him, Lafond was not going to let me stay on with Remedes. I was counting on Dufour's support to achieve my aim. Lafond's last statement had, however, given rise to serious doubts in my mind about Dufour's ability to help me. He was clearly not in a position to overrule the Director General.

'Bonjour, Madame Masmejean,' I greeted Dufour's secretary.

'Bonjour. What brings you here? I hope it's not to see the boss.'

'That's precisely what I am here for. Is he too busy?'

'No, not too busy, but he is in a foul mood again today. The day began with a meeting of senior officers taken by the

Director General as every Wednesday does. Raymond came back in an awful temper.'

'Do you know what could have gone wrong?'

'Not exactly. But he came back cursing Monsieur Lafond. That's not unusual. You know they don't get along and that's to put it mildly.'

'Could you please tell him I am here and would like to see him for a few minutes?'

'Why do you insist on seeing him on the days he is upset?'

I knew that Dufour's anger today was most likely in favour of my cause. But it was not clear if it was a manifestation of his determination to override the block put forth by Lafond or a sign of his frustration at not being able to help me.

'I'll take a chance,' I said.

'If you must,' said Mme Masmejean and informed Dufour of my arrival. I was called in immediately.

'I am afraid I don't have good news for you,' Dufour was forthright.

'That's disappointing.'

'It's this Gaston who spoiled whatever little chance of success we had. As soon as I broached the subject, he pounced upon me. You know our case was quite weak. Gaston's strong opposition ensured its quick demise. I tried to explain that we could use you fruitfully here and that even in your absence, our project in India could take off, albeit with some extra effort by the chemists in your father's company. The Director General backed Gaston. What hurt me the most was Gaston's accusation that I was working against the interests of Remedes. I can't bear being accused of insincerity to my own company.' Dufour's pent-up feelings gushed out like lava from a volcano.

'I am sorry Monsieur; you had to face an embarrassing situation because of me.'

'Well I have always stood by my friends. And look at this Gaston. He always scoffs at my love-life and broadcasts his trust in the puritanical virtue of remaining faithful to a single woman. No wonder he has stuck on to his wife who has bloated to the size of a fattened pig over the years. And yet when I mentioned the reason for your request, he said Remedes could not afford to be compassionate in such matters and must look to its own interests. He is such a bundle of contradictions.' Dufour's tirade against Lafond was unending.

I didn't know what more to say.

'Have you met Gaston?' Dufour asked.

'Yes, Monsieur, it was a very unpleasant meeting.'

'I hope he didn't humiliate you too much.'

'Well, he said I was trying to swindle Remedes. But that was nothing new. Each time I have met him, I have seen him humiliating someone or the other.'

'The man is utterly mean. I know your case is weak and not entirely in the interests of Remedes. But I wish I could keep you here just to teach Gaston a lesson. It's a pity I can't do so in the face of the Director General's support to Gaston. Anyway, what are you planning to do now? Can you get over this affair of yours?'

'I wish I could do that, but I just can't think of leaving Emilie behind.'

'Then take her with you to India.'

'She is the only child of her mother and finds it difficult to leave her mother alone here.'

'Now let me repeat this Lalit in the hope that you understand the point I made the first time we spoke of this matter. This woman of yours may be the only child of her mother. But she is not the only woman in this world. Believe me you will find many others like her and even better. When you fall in love for the first time, the care and affection of your woman overwhelm you. But as you go along, you realise that most of them are caring and affectionate. Besides, change is always better than a static and stale situation in life.'

'I don't think any woman can match Emilie. Moreover, I am committed to her. What would happen to her if I leave her midway?'

'I am sure she will find another man.'

'I wish it were as simple for her to find another man and for me to find another woman.'

'I am sure you will realise one day that what I say is correct, but that day may take some time to dawn. In the meanwhile, we have a problem on our hands.' Dufour paused for a few seconds and then added, 'I can see only one way out.'

'What is it?' My eyes lit up at the thought of a way out of the maze I was caught in.

'You have no personal commitment to Remedes. It's your father's company that has commitments to us. I would hate to do it to my family. But if you are desperate, you could try to get a job here with another company. With your training, you could get one, even though they may not pay you as much as to a local person because of the hassle of getting you a work permit.'

'Could you help me in getting a job?

'Not if I could help it. I would hate to betray Remedes. But this Gaston has completely put me off. I could discreetly talk to some people who may consider you for a job. But I would once again urge you to give a careful consideration to the matter. Even if you forget about the Remedes production line in India, you should not ignore the sentiments of your family.'

'Thank you for your concern, Monsieur. I shall think over this matter and may come back for your help.'

'Good luck to you.'

I returned to the factory around lunchtime and spent a restless day at work. Phone calls to the office and residence of Emilie revealed that she was still not back. By the evening, I was mentally exhausted. As our production shift drew to a close, I stared out of the window. One could see nothing but dull and drab buildings. Lost in my thoughts, I didn't realise that the bell signalling the end of our shift had gone off and everyone was moving out.

'Which world are you lost in?' It was Georges, our unit in-charge.

'I am going through a serious personal crisis.' The words just escaped my mouth. I was in desperate need to talk to someone.

'I can make that out. Your eyes are bloodshot. I hope you don't have fever.'

'No it's just intense mental activity. And yet, I have no solution to my predicament.'

'What is your predicament?'

'Let me not burden you with it.'

'O, come on! It's no burden at all. You must talk to someone.'

I looked around. Some workers were still moving around.

'We don't have to talk here. Let's have dinner together. Be my guest this evening.'

'Look I don't want to hassle you,' I protested.

'It's high time you stopped being formal. My wife is away to her hometown and I am eating out anyway. I am inviting you to join me unless you have something better lined up. The last thing you need is to sit back and brood at home.'

'It's so nice of you Georges.' The invitation came as a godsend for me.

We went to a nearby Algerian restaurant and started off with beer.

'Now tell me what is bothering you,' Georges enquired.

'Well, I am in love with a woman. She cannot leave her mother here to accompany me to India. I am finding it difficult to stay on here.' I explained the complexity of my situation.

'Poor you! I can see your predicament.'

'Would you say my family has a better claim on me than this woman?' The question had troubled me the whole afternoon.

'I wouldn't say that. It's a question of *your* life. Remedes operations in India will carry on somehow without you. But if you leave this woman before you have your fill of her, her memory would torment you all your life.'

'How long does it take one to have one's fill of a woman?'

'That's a difficult question to answer. I am fifty-five now and have been seriously involved with three women. The first one was an English girl, barely twenty. I had escaped to England during the Second World War. We had a frenzied affair for three or four months. And then she suddenly disappeared. Some said she had died in an air raid. Her memory still torments me. I had obviously not had my fill of her. I was then married to a woman for about two years. She was utterly selfish and worse still insincere. We separated and I hardly ever think of her. Then came my wife. We hit it off so well that every day brings greater dependence on each other. I don't think I'll ever end up having my fill of her.' Georges laughed as he signalled to the owner to take our order. We both ordered Couscous,

'Let me tell you Georges, the woman I love falls in the category of your wife,' I said.

'How do you know?'

'Well I have known her long enough.'

'How long?'

'Around nine months now.'

'I can't tell you which category she belongs to. However, I can clearly see that you haven't had your fill of her.'

When we parted, Georges said, 'Remember, don't take this matter lightly and don't give undue importance to your family obligations.'

My attempt to doze off that night proved to be futile. Not having anything else to do, I walked up to the phone and dialled Emilie's home number in Paris. She answered the phone at the very first ring.

'Emilie, where have you been all this while?'

'Mother was a little unwell and I had to prolong my stay.'

'What was the matter with her? I hope you could talk to her about us?'

'Yes, I did.'

'What was her response?'

'She is strongly opposed to the idea of my going away to India. Her reaction was hysterical. She developed high blood pressure and I had to stay on. In fact, I have brought her along for a few days.'

'Emilie, God only knows what He has in store for us. My attempt to stay on with Remedes has also come a cropper. Could you please let me meet your mother? I may be able to persuade her to let you go.'

'I doubt if you could convince her where I failed. It would be better if you let me continue with my efforts,' Emilie said.

'Emilie, we don't have much time. Let me see her just once.'

'All right, come around six thirty tomorrow evening. I'll be back from work by then.'

The phone talk had left me completely depressed. All the doors were getting shut on us slowly.

What a day, I thought, as I slumped into my bed – only to keep awake.

Dealing with Madame Martin was a daunting task under the best of circumstances. Doing so in my situation – asking for her daughter's hand in marriage in the face of her outright opposition – was nothing short of a nightmare. My heart was pounding as I entered Emilie's studio. Her eyes were full of apprehension. I gave her as reassuring a look as I could in my own nervous condition. Madame Martin was sitting in a dining chair. As I came in her line of sight, she turned her face away from me.

'Bonjour, Madame Martin,' said I.

There was no response.

'Bonjour, Madame Martin,' I repeated a little louder.

There was still no response.

'Madame, I have come to discuss an important matter with you,' I made bold to broach my delicate subject without waiting for her response to my salutation.

At this, she turned her face sharply towards me. Her eyes were bloodshot.

'I know what you want and I think you have my response through my daughter. If you had even a speck of sensitivity, you would have lain off by now,' she did not mince her words.

'But Emilie loves me and will not be able to stay without me', I pleaded.

'I am sure left to herself she can stay very well without you. But you are bent upon ruining her life.'

Emilie tried to intervene but was cut short. 'Let me sort him out,' said Madame Martin.

'But you can't be so heartless,' I was losing my patience.

'Yes I am heartless because I want to save my daughter from the travails of living in an alien environment. Yes I am heartless because I want to save my daughter from certain disaster that would await her in her marriage with you. Look, who is calling me heartless,' Madame Martin was shrieking, 'a man who wants to take my only child thousands of miles away. Oh God! Oh God! Why have you brought this upon me?' Saying this, Madame Martin slumped in her chair.

'Oh my God!' both Emilie and I exclaimed simultaneously.

Emilie rushed to the phone to call the emergency medical service – 'SOS Medecin' – as I tried to prop Madame Martin up.

She seemed to be in a state of semi-consciousness and was muttering something to herself. Emilie looked at me with a guilty gaze as if cursing herself for her mother's condition.

A doctor and his paramedic arrived in a few minutes. They examined the lady who by this time had recovered somewhat.

'Nothing serious,' the doctor declared, 'Her blood pressure is quite high.'

Emilie showed him the medicines Madame Martin was taking for hypertension.

'Let her continue with these pills and take plenty of rest. Try to keep her away from anxiety,' the doctor's instructions were clear.

Emilie looked at me as the doctor and his assistant left.

'I know I must leave,' said I moving towards the door. Emilie hugged me as soon as we were out of her mother's sight.

I looked at her face. Two tears had rolled out of her eyes and were sitting like pearls on her cheeks.

Yet another door had banged shut on Emilie and me.

*

Raymond Dufour was as charming as ever on phone when I called him the following day.

'So you have come against a dead end, haven't you Lalit?' He was quick to guess my dilemma.

'You are right, Monsieur.'

'You are sure you can't leave this woman – what is her name? – ah yes – this Emilie of yours.'

'Monsieur, I have told you I can't live without her. Her mother is strongly against my marrying her and her going away to India. I must stay on here in the hope that Emilie's mother would relent in letting me marry her on the condition that we stay on in France.'

'God! What sort of men have you produced,' Raymond sounded exasperated, 'but my dear Lalit is not the first of this kind,' he consoled himself, doing some loud thinking on the phone.

'Have you given the matter a careful thought?'

'Yes, Monsieur I have,' said I.

'Well then let me speak to my friend Laurent in Pharma France. He had mentioned to me a few days ago that he was looking for a beginner for his production line. Mind you their line is much smaller than ours. But there is no harm in trying.'

'I shall be eternally grateful to you, Monsieur.'

I had called Dufour from my home. It was an hour before I reached the Remedes office after withdrawing some money from my bank. The receptionist told me that Dufour wanted to see me urgently. My spirits rose. Maybe there is an opening, I thought.

'Where have you been all this while?' Dufour asked. 'I tried your residence but no one would answer. Anyway, rush to the Pharma office at this address,' he said, handing over a piece of paper to me.' Laurent is right now interviewing some youngsters. He was initially reluctant to consider you. Work permit hassles, he said. But at my insistence he has agreed to have a look at you. So go and try your luck.'

I took the metro to the Pharma office.

Compared to the Remedes Headquarters, the Pharma office was miniscule. It was a big hall divided into cubicles with wooden partitions.

'Oui, Monsieur,' the receptionist sitting close to the main entrance looked at me inquiringly.

'I am here for an interview for a job in your company,' said I.

'Oh la la! Not another one,' she exclaimed. 'There is after all just one job and you are the eighth person to drop by for an interview. Anyway take a seat.'

I took a seat in the waiting area and surveyed the scene. There was a young man and two young ladies – apparently all candidates for the same job. The remaining of the eight mentioned by the receptionist appeared to have left after the interview. Both the girls were dressed provocatively, their bosoms nearly spilling out of their tight plunging neckline tops. Rather glamorous chemists, I mused. 'Would I stand any chance against them?' – the thought crossed my mind, particularly if Laurent is like his friend Raymond Dufour. Getting a job here was a matter of life and death for me and there was just one job going. The odds were heavily against me and something as trivial as the plunging neckline of the girls' tops seemed to emerge as a formidable barrier between me and my goal. It was a crawling one hour before my turn came.

'You are?' Laurent looked at me. He appeared to be a pleasant person like Dufour.

'Monsieur Dufour sent me to you,' I replied.

'Ah you are Monsieur K-ha....,' Laurent got stuck trying to read my name from a piece of paper.

'Khanna, Monsieur,' I helped him.

'Ah yes Monsieur Kha-nn-a,' he still had difficulty pronouncing my name. Look I have just one job and I would much rather avoid work permit issues. But my good friend Raymond insisted on my seeing you and swore by your professional competence. So I agreed to meet you. Now give me a description of the apprenticeship you did at Remedes.'

The next twenty minutes were spent in a recap of my training. Laurent interrupted me repeatedly to ask questions, no doubt to test my knowledge. He seemed impressed with my performance.

'How much money would you expect?' he asked me in the end.

'Whatever you consider appropriate,' I did not want to give him any cause for offence.

'Look I could offer you something like eight thousand Francs a month. Besides I shall have to tap my resources in the bureaucracy to get you a work permit. I hope this is fine by you.'

I knew that a person with my qualifications could earn around ten thousand Francs a month. But I had no choice.

'That should be perfectly fine,' I responded immediately.

'Well, then you could start from the first of October. But come again on Monday. We must initiate your work permit formalities. You could come around ten.'

'Merci infiniment Monsieur,' I couldn't control my joy as I left the Pharma office. I went to the nearest public phone booth to thank Dufour.

'I am very glad for you, though I still strongly oppose your philosophy about women,' he had a hearty laugh.

*

I called Emilie as soon as I reached home.

'How is your mother?'

'She is fine and leaving for Poitiers tomorrow evening with a friend who is going by car.'

'Emie I have good news. I have got a job with a company courtesy Dufour and can stay on here. We must meet as soon as your mother leaves tomorrow.'

'Lali you haven't done well in getting a job here. Think of the disappointment it would cause your family.'

I was not surprised at Emilie's reaction. With her maturity, she had all along acted as an antidote to my impulsive nature.

'Why don't you come tomorrow and we will talk about it,' said I. I was sure I could convince her of the desirability of my decision.

'Okay, I shall see you tomorrow. I'll be there around seven in the evening.'

I called my landlord to ask if I could continue to retain my studio. He said he had not lined up another tenant and would be happy to renew the lease with me once the earlier one signed with Remedes came to an end the following week.

I poured myself a beer and settled down in front of the TV.

The phone rang. It was a long distance call. My brother Udai was on the line.

'Lalit I hear you plan to stay on there because of a woman,' he sounded agitated.

'Who told you?'

'Gaston called me. He was furious. Said you hadn't confirmed your departure despite his warning. He said your stay would be a breach of contract. That doesn't bother me as much as how Papa would take your decision. We didn't tell you earlier but he suffered a heart attack about four weeks ago.'

I burst out crying.

'Don't worry; he is out of danger now and well on his way to recovery. But you must realise he will not be able to devote much time to the factory any more. I can't run it alone. You must grow up Lalit. You must assume your responsibility.'

By this time my head was a jumble of emotions and confusion.

'Please wish Papa a speedy recovery,' is all I could say.

'Look Lalit, Gaston told me they have a booking for you on the Monday Air India flight. I hope to see you back here early Tuesday morning unless I hear from you to the contrary and I hope and pray to God I don't hear from you to the contrary. You don't have to worry. I haven't mentioned anything to Mama and Papa.'

Udai was only four years older than me and as we had grown up together, we had learnt to keep each other's secrets.

I was sobbing uncontrollably.

'Look don't disappoint us. See you coming Tuesday and don't worry, we are taking good care of Papa,' said Udai as he closed the call.

I sat transfixed in front of the TV. The eight o' clock news had started on TF1 channel. However, my thoughts were elsewhere – with my father. My mother was a strict disciplinarian, while my father, who because of his professional commitments got very little time with us, always pampered Udai and me whenever he could devote some time to us. He was very gentle and soft spoken. He was honest to a fault. He had come into big money only around ten years ago, but had never let us have a sense of deprivation. All festivals were celebrated in our home with a great deal of fervour. For a number of days before *Diwali*, he would take us to the market every evening to build up our stock of firecrackers. Whenever anyone at home was sick, he would sit up the whole night, if required, regardless of a gruelling schedule the following day. He was equally devoted to his patients. During his days of medical practice, he would come back home very late because he gave all the time needed to every patient. More than anyone else in the family, I was emotionally dependent on him. I would take all my problems to him and always come back with a solution and emotional reassurance. He made Udai and me feel like the greatest boys in the world. Our smallest achievements were touted around. Our failures were blamed on circumstances or judges of our performance. He would quote instances from his own life when he had moved on to achieve success despite failures on the way. He was a pillar of strength for all of us. And now he was in need of his family's help. He needed support, more so of his sons for whom he had done so much. I would no longer be able to or wish to take my problems to him. I would have to grow up as Udai had said and face the world on my own. I could not be selfish with a man who had been so selfless all his life. I must go back to India. My mind was made up.

The last door had banged shut on Emilie and me.

The following day was a Saturday. My decision to leave for India on Monday meant that I would have to tie up a number of loose ends on Saturday itself. I called my landlord first thing in the morning. He was surprised at my quick change of mind but was satisfied when I explained my circumstances. He came over to take inventory of the furniture and furnishings in the studio. He pointed out several instances of damage to the property, supposedly caused by me and said I would have to shell out three thousand francs as compensation. Such claims by landlords were common. My plea that many of the defects were too insignificant and the others had been there when I took possession of the studio fell on deaf ears. It was following some haggling that we settled the matter at a thousand francs. I spent some time in collecting my personal belongings for packing.

I then went to the market to pick up LPs of some of my favourite songs. The purchase having been made, I wandered aimlessly along the streets of Paris savouring the lively atmosphere of this beautiful city. I walked down from Arc de Triomphe to Place de la Concorde and then back to the Arc. I took the Metro to Rue Mouffetard in Quartier Latin and then walked across to Ile de La Cite – all landmarks witness to the blossoming of love between Emilie and me. Cities, I thought, live on for thousands of years witness to momentous events and changing course of history, that are recorded by historians for posterity. What the cities also witness, but what never gets recorded, are the lives of their ordinary dwellers who weave their little bonds of love and friendship and family ties that assume a pre-eminent place in their existence and then pass into oblivion as each generation moves on. The struggle of these ordinary people to fashion a happy life for themselves and their loved ones remains unsung. I was leaving Emilie behind not knowing what future held for us. Would I ever meet her again or would the part of my life spent with her just die, smothered by our circumstances?

I was back home by six. Emilie walked in around seven as promised.

'Which company have you got a job with?' she enquired.

'That's an old story,' I said to a wide-eyed Emilie and then went on to narrate what had transpired after my previous evening's call to her. She looked dazed.

I knew she had been opposed to my staying on in France against the wishes of my family. But I also knew that she even more abhorred the thought of separation from me. There was just no easy answer.

'Let me show you some new LPs I bought today,' I said to lighten the atmosphere and passed on the LPs one by one to Emilie.

These were songs we had grown fond of together. I could see she was trying to fight back tears.

We had dinner at a restaurant in Quartier Latin and danced late into the night to forget our worries. It was 2 am when we came back to my studio.

'Let's get some sleep, there will be plenty of packing work tomorrow,' I proposed.

We were soon in bed.

'Lali you won't forget me?' Emilie asked.

'Do you have any doubts?'

'No.' said Emilie, 'But I'll miss you each second.'

'I'll miss you too Emie.'

Words of mutual commitment and more words of mutual commitment were our only source of solace.

Sunday was a bright sunny day. I spent most of the morning in packing my personal belongings. I had for quite some time wanted to buy a few paintings for my sister-in-law. Emilie suggested a visit to Montmartre, where at Place du Tertre or the artists' square close to the Sacred Heart Basilica, I might be able to get some good paintings. We passed by Place Pigalle to reach our destination. The place was relatively tranquil at that time of the day but would come to life in the evening. Bright neon signs, including the famous red windmill of Moulin Rouge, touted the wares of the place ranging from peep shows to strip clubs, blue movies, cabarets and sex gadgets. 'Sexy girls', 'Super Sexy girls', 'Realise your fantasies' – the neon signs cried out in an endeavour to outdo each other. A wave of visitors would descend on this area every evening. Tourists desirous of seeing the place out of curiosity or others out to fulfil their sexual desires. The area offered unmatched sexual pleasures or unequalled sexual depravity, depending upon how you looked at it – as a liberated soul or as a puritan. A friend had told me that even puritans visited the place at least once before rejecting it as a den of evil. It had taken Burhan two visits with Sunil and me before pronouncing that it was a refuge of the depraved. Now that I was on the verge of leaving Paris, places that I would have passed by without so much as giving a thought only a few days ago were evoking the countless recollections of my association with this enthralling city.

Located on the Montmartre hill, the highest point in Paris, the Sacred Heart Basilica is at once a religious place and a famous tourist spot. The area – with its panoramic view of Paris, old houses, traditional streets, lively cafés and above all the Basilica and the artists' square – is always teeming with tourists. The Basilica, built in Romano-Byzantine style at a cost of 40 million francs – a staggering amount at that time – from 1875 to 1914, sits like a piece of jewel on the hill especially on a clear sunny day. The place was as lively as ever when Emilie and I reached there. We passed by a few street musicians playing popular tunes. A man in a suit, his face, neck and hands painted chalk-white, stood like a statue on a wooden block without the slightest movement and without blinking his eyes. People were throwing money into a container lying near him. Some tourists would stop by to take his picture or to get themselves photographed with him. Vendors were busy selling cold drinks, snacks and candy floss. We went inside the church with its impressive mosaic of Christ with outstretched arms – reportedly one of the world's largest mosaics.

I lit a candle and offered prayers.

'What did you ask for?' Emilie enquired.

'For you.'

'Do you think such prayers have any worth?'

'Let's not start this debate again,' I cut her short.

We proceeded to the artists' square. We were pestered by a person who wanted to cut out my profile from a piece of paper. He wanted thirty Francs for the job. I said I was not interested. He nonetheless followed us and reduced the price first to twenty-five, then twenty and then fifteen Francs. When I still refused his offer, he proceeded to cut out my profile anyway and completed the task in a jiffy. I was highly impressed with his work and readily paid fifteen Francs to buy the profile. The paintings were expensive and I could pick up only one. An artist offered to do a pencil portrait of Emilie. She was hesitant but settled down for the task following my persuasion. The portrait was a masterpiece catching Emilie's charm even better than a coloured photograph. I marvelled at the speed and dexterity of the artists.

I gave Emilie my profile cutout and she gave me her portrait.

We went into a café near Place du Tertre for a drink. We had been there earlier on a few occasions in happier times. But today was a different day. The gaiety around passed us by. Emilie and I sat with our drinks, staring into the air in search of numerous memories of the past.

During our travel back home by the Metro, I asked Emilie, 'When shall we meet again?'

'Lali you know I can't live very long without you. I shall continue my effort to convince my mother to let me go and as soon as she agrees, I shall be with you.'

'As soon as she agrees,' I repeated.

'Let's not lose hope,' Emilie said.

I nodded in agreement.

Monday morning was spent in saying goodbyes at the Remedes factory and office. I rang up Laurent to say I was unable to join his company. I profusely thanked Dufour for all his help. I had a brief meeting with Lafond. He barely looked up from the papers he was studying when I went to say goodbye.

'Work hard in your father's factory,' is all he said.

The Air India flight to Delhi was at six in the evening. Emilie and I took a taxi to the Orly airport. After check in, I didn't go immediately for emigration so as to spend the maximum possible time with Emilie. Boarding was now being announced. I gave her a tight hug. I looked into her big blue eyes. They were brimming with tears. My own eyes had become hazy.

'Au revoir – till we meet again,' I said. I liked this French expression. You never said you were leaving a person for good but only till you met him or her again.

I quickly went through emigration. I was to walk straight, in Emilie's line of sight, for about twenty feet before turning left to go to my boarding gate. During that short walk, I looked back nearly ten times – each time to find Emilie waiving her hand with a faint smile on her face. Finally she was out of my sight. In a few more minutes, the plane had lifted off the ground taking me on my journey far away from the woman I had come to love more than my life.

Homecoming is always a thrilling experience and it was so for me regardless of the deep melancholic note of separation from Emilie. My mother and Udai were at the airport to receive me.

'You have lost so much weight,' was the first observation my mother made on seeing me.

'You must be joking Mama, he has put on some weight,' said Udai and he was absolutely right. I had indeed put on a few kilos during a year's stay in France.

'Don't try to console me,' my mother retorted. 'I knew he would not relish the tasteless food you get in those countries.

Anyway now that he is back, I shall make sure he goes back to his normal self.'

'Mama, would you ever change!' I said as I hugged her.

My father was already up by the time we reached home.

'How have you been, son?' he asked taking me in his arms

'I have been fine. How are you Papa?'

'Well, as you see I am fit as ever.'

'I was so worried about you.'

'Worried about what?'

'Udai told me everything.'

'Ah, this stupid fellow. I had asked him not to mention anything to you. Well it was a mild heart attack. My heart has to grow weaker with age. I am after all sixty now. But so long as two strong hearts beat in my sons for me, I have nothing to be concerned about.' His response was as comforting as ever. He would have been heartbroken if I had not come back.

It was breakfast time and the whole family was around the table. Little Sanjiv was toddling around, giggling and going 'Sasa' each time he saw me. He had obviously been told that his *Chacha* was coming home.

My mother had prepared my favourite aloo-paranthas. She served them with homemade butter. As I was busy relishing the paranthas, to my horror she brought the largest available glass full of milk for me. I kept quiet thinking I would negotiate the quantity to be drunk with her later. The next I found her cracking open a raw egg into the glass. 'Oh no!' I said to myself, 'There we go again.' Udai and I had been made to drink innumerable tasteless egg flips during our younger days.

'Mama what are you doing?' I protested. Udai gave me an amused look. Since his marriage, he had been by and large spared mother's foodie attention.

'Egg flip is very essential for growing children,' she was ready with an answer.

'You think I am a growing child. I am twenty-four,' I said, emphasising each of the last four words.

'Yes I know you are twenty four,' she replied. 'But this is essential to protect you against infections. September-October are bad months. Too many viral infections in the air.' My objection had been overruled.

'But Mama, he is no longer a child,' Udai came to my help.

'I know he is no more exactly a child. I would be very happy to see him married so that his wife takes on the burden of looking after him as Shobha has done for you.'

I didn't want to discuss the dimension of marriage my mother had added to the food saga. 'All right Mama I shall drink it,' I said resignedly.

'That's like a good boy,' my father chipped in, partly out of appreciation for my having given in to my mother's wish and partly to pull my leg.

The egg flip done with, I was made to eat some seasonal fruits before the breakfast came to an end.

Udai was leaving for the factory. My eyes instinctively fell on the letterbox when I went out to see him off. It was empty. Emilie had promised to write to me twice a week.' It's too early to expect a letter from her, silly,' I told myself. In any case I had asked her to send letters at our factory address, as these were more likely to escape undue attention there.

Not having been able to get much sleep on the flight, I slept most of the day. By the time dinner was over, my mother had turned me into a stuffed turkey.

An after-dinner family chitchat was a normal affair in our home.

The early bird that my father was, he would feel very groggy by then, but would sit around, occasionally making a comment or two but most of the time dozing. However on this occasion he was sent promptly to bed because of his need for rest. The conversation was mostly about France. My father had visited that country on a few occasions. The others had not been there and were curious to know everything about it.

It was nearly twelve. Sanjiv was coughing in his sleep. Shobha went to look after him. Mother also decided to call it a day.

'Who is this woman?' Udai asked me finding me alone.

'Her name is Emilie. She is a medical researcher.'

'An appropriate profession for the family,' Udai said.

I knew what he was referring to. Nearly everyone in our family was connected with the medical profession. My maternal grandfather was a doctor too and my mother claimed a sound knowledge of basic medicine. She would often maintain unjustifiably that when Udai and I were children, she had treated our common ailments mostly on her own. Shobha was a clinical psychologist by training, though now a housewife.

'Do you intend marrying her?' Udai asked.

'Yes.'

'Would she be joining you here?'

'She has a dilemma. Her mother is against her marrying me and coming to India.'

'I suppose if she loves you, she would defy her mother.'

'She is madly in love with me, but things are not that simple. Her father and only brother died some years ago. She is hesitant to leave her mother alone in France.'

'So?' Udai enquired.

What options did I have under the circumstances? I had been tossing this question around in my mind for a long time and had no answer.

'Let's call it a day,' I said to postpone consideration of this tricky issue.

I had been back home for two weeks and had been sharing Udai's work at the factory that was working in two shifts. He would go for work early in the morning and come back around six in the evening. I would go a little later and come back late in the evening.

'Come back early today,' my mother shouted after me as I left. 'Sachdeva uncle and family are in Delhi and are coming this evening to visit us.'

'Okay, Mama,' I said.

The Sachdevas were our neighbours when almost fourteen years ago we lived in Ludhiana where my father was practising medicine. Their son Shantanu was Udai's age and their daughter Shalini, a year or two my junior. Our parents were close friends. Contacts between the two families had become occasional once we moved to Delhi. I had seen Mr and Mrs Sachdeva some two years ago, but had not met Shantanu and Shalini for a long time.

Bahadur, our Nepalese messenger came to leave a sheaf of papers in my office. Looked like some boring statistical sheets of production figures. The machinery imported from France had been installed and our Remedes production line was slowly picking up.

'Where were you? I didn't see you earlier,' I asked Bahadur.

'I had gone home, Saheb. Came back yesterday.'

'You look very pleased with life.'

'I am so glad to see you, Saheb,' Bahadur had refined the art of sycophancy to hitherto unknown heights. He was illiterate but had a sound commonsense and was very sharp at gauging what would please his employers.

'Now shut up. Your happiness is not all about my coming back.'

'Saheb, I got married and have brought my wife along.'

'Well there you are. I knew there was some special reason for you to beam ear to ear. Is your wife happy in India?'

'She has been here just for a day, Saheb, but she is thrilled. She is excited about this big city. She is so happy about the fan in our quarter and the cold water she gets from the factory cooler.'

'Good. Keep her happy and stop drinking too much.'

'Never again, Saheb,' said Bahadur touching his earlobes with the tips of his index fingers.

I flipped through the papers left behind by Bahadur. My eyes fell on the envelope I had been waiting for since I arrived in India – a letter from Emilie. I hurriedly opened it and read it without lifting my eyes even once. Each word reflected the pain of separation. 'After seeing you off, I came back home, cried for a long time and went off to sleep out of sheer mental exhaustion, but only to get up the next morning with the unbearable thought of separation from you. Nothing has changed. I work, I eat and I sleep. But my life is hollow just because you are not here. I occasionally go out for walks along the Seine. I wish you were by my side. Lali, I shall continue my effort to persuade my mother to let me go. I'll join you as soon as she agrees,' she had written.

'As soon as she agrees,' I repeated the words to myself. 'What if she never agrees?' – the thought hit my head like a hammer. I quickly pushed it aside before it could overpower me. I read the letter over and over again. I was happy to receive a message of love and commitment from Emilie, but it had also sharpened my pain.

Caught up in the rush of work, I could get back home only around seven in the evening.

'Why are you so late?' my mother shouted as I entered the house. 'I asked you to come back early today,'

'Mama it's only seven,' I protested.

'Yes, but Sachdevas should be here anytime and you are yet to dress up properly to meet them.'

I ran to the toilet without answering her.

When I came out after a shower, I could hear chitchat in the drawing room. The Sachdevas had already arrived. My mother came out hurriedly. One look at me and she disapproved of my casual dress. She insisted that I wear a suit. I was puzzled. Our relationship with the Sachdevas was not formal enough to warrant my wearing a suit to meet them.

'Mama you don't need to be in a stiff suit to meet old friends.' I protested.

'They have been here for half an hour and you are nowhere to be seen. Anyway, at least put on a good jacket and come fast to the drawing room.' Being tense on such occasions was not unusual for my mother.

Mr and Mrs Sachdeva gave me a hearty welcome. Both Shantanu and Shalini had changed a great deal since I last met them. Shalini, a gawky little girl, had become a tall and pretty woman. She blushed when I greeted her. An awkward silence ensued which was broken by my father, 'You don't have to feel shy children just because you haven't met for a long time. Remember the days when you were all part of a nuisance syndicate against your parents.'

'Not only against you,' I corrected my father. 'Don't you remember that Shalini used to give me a run for my money?' Everyone laughed and Shalini blushed again.

'She is the same lively creature. Give her some time to open up,' said Mrs Sachdeva as Shalini buried her face in her hands.

The conversation centred on our days in Ludhiana. Tea and snacks were served. 'How was your training in France?' Mr Sachdeva asked.

'It was very interesting. I am now an expert on the production line that we have recently set up.'

'What else could one expect from Dr Khanna's son?' Mr Sachdeva flattered my father.

'Shantanu is by God's grace a much sought-after doctor in Ludhiana and Shalini, my dear little girl, has just completed MA in English with flying colours,' Mrs Sachdeva was as immodest as ever.

'Well, I am an old fashioned person and believe that the best place for girls is at home as good wives and mothers,' Mrs Sachdeva continued. 'But we insisted that Shalini got good education even though she doesn't plan to pursue any career. Mind you I have not allowed her education to interfere with her training in household chores. Visit us in Ludhiana and you can taste wonderful dishes made by Shalini – butter chicken, bhuna gosht ...' Mrs Sachdeva rattled off a long list of dishes as she and my mother looked on affectionately at Shalini who was now blushing for the umpteenth time.

'That reminds me, you must have dinner with us,' my mother said.

'No, *bahenji*, I mentioned to you on phone that Sachdeva Sahib and I have another commitment. But the children must have dinner together. They are meeting after a long time. Perhaps they can go out to a nice restaurant,' Mrs Sachdeva suggested.

'Shobha and I have to go to a friend's wedding anniversary party,' said Udai.

'Then let Shantanu, Shalini and Lalit have dinner together,' my mother chipped in.

'Let's go to Casa Medici in Taj Mansingh,' Shantanu proposed.

Shortly thereafter, the three of us were on our way to Taj Mansingh.

We had barely started looking at the menu cards when a waiter approached us.

'Is Mr Shantanu Sachdeva amongst you?' he asked.'Yes, I am Shantanu.'

'Sir, there is a phone call for you,' the waiter said.

Shantanu walked down to the restaurant desk to take the call. When he came back, he was very apologetic and said he had to leave immediately. His father was planning to buy a property in Delhi and was scheduled to have dinner with the seller to finalise the deal. Everything had been tied up, but Mr Sachdeva had called to say that the seller had raised some last minute problems and he wanted Shantanu around to resolve the same. Shantanu asked us to enjoy our meal and said he would be back as soon as possible. He was not going too far, he said. His parents were meeting the seller in Connaught Place.

Shantanu left. Shalini dug her gaze into the menu card.

'What will you drink?' I asked to break the heavy silence that had followed Shantanu's departure. She lifted her gaze in response to my question.

'Will you have Coke?' I asked. 'I know you were very fond of Coke as a child.'

'Not as much as you were,' she said with a smile as the memory of our childhood brightened her up.'Do you remember when you drank too much of Coke at a wedding and were found throwing up in the garden?'

'Yes, I shall never forget that day, particularly the shouting I got from Papa. And you greedy, don't you remember the day when you ate too much of burfi and were terribly sick.' Shalini and I had been partners in many crimes.'Yes, of course. How can I forget that day? It's just that my tummy warned me many times to stop eating but I couldn't resist my palate.'

Shalini burst out laughing and said, 'Didn't you once climb a mango tree too high and were then unable to get down?'

'Yeah, but you had egged me on to climb that high to pluck raw mangoes for you and had started crying when I was having difficulty getting down, bringing my hysterical parents to the scene. And, of course, the worst was the tight slap that I got from my father once he had brought me down and all this for no fault of mine,' I complained.

'Now don't blame me for your own naughty deeds,' Shalini retorted.

'This is grossly unfair,' I protested. 'You can't call me naughty. Most of the time it was your ideas that landed me in trouble. Remember when we were both quarantined for two days for playing football in the afternoon sun in June. You had been the spirit behind that football game which brought us so much of misery.'

'As if you were an angel and didn't want to play in the sun,' Shalini said in a mocking tone. 'You used to rope me in because you didn't have sufficient number of boys for your game.'

We both had a hearty laugh. Shalini was right. As a child, I found it difficult to sit still at home on summer afternoons. It was simply too boring. My father had a long afternoon break from his practice in summer and my parents had a siesta every day before he went back to work for the evening shift when it started becoming a little cooler. Our parents were keen that both Udai and I also took a siesta. But sleep stayed miles away from us. Our playing any indoor game was out of question, as it would disturb our parents. So we were forced everyday to lie down and shut our eyes in the hope that sleep would oblige us! Lying down with eyes shut for two hours is not an easy task, especially for a child. Udai and I would steal a glance every now and then at the grandfather clock on the opposite wall, after what we thought had been an eternity, only to find that the minutes hand had moved only by five minutes. Invariably, both of us were left using sign language within a few minutes to amuse ourselves. Such interaction often resulted in a chuckle inviting a sharp reprimand from one of the parents and a temporary ban on the sign language, which resumed as soon as our parents were asleep again. On occasions, we would slip out to play in the courtyard of our house, joined by other children similarly tormented by their parents, and slip in before our parents could detect our escapade. On the fateful day, Shantanu and Udai had gone to see a movie with some friends. Shalini had alerted me to the possibility of a football game post lunch. So both of us escaped from our respective houses to converge in our courtyard for what was to be a short-lived football match involving just two players. We were soon detected and quarantined inside our respective homes for forty-eight hours through a joint decision of our fathers. It was an inhuman punishment, we had thought at that time. Our misfortune had been mitigated by occasional outings allowed by our mothers during the quarantine period when our fathers were away. These were engineered through emotional blackmail.

'Well, I am still in love with the game,' I said. 'Do you also play football?'

'No!' Shalini was emphatic, 'I am grown up now.'

I realised the stupidity of my question. In the excitement of talking of our childhood, I had momentarily forgotten that Shalini was now a young lady and not the same eight year old, I had known in Ludhiana. My gaze suddenly got fixed on her lovely face. She was not only very beautiful, but also had a very pleasant personality. Seeing me staring at her, she looked away.

The food had arrived. She ate very little, saying she needed to watch her weight. We talked mostly of old times. I asked her what she planned to do after her MA and hoped that her parents would not rush her into a marriage.

'Well they certainly won't rush me into anything, but they feel that I should get married now.'

'I can tell you, they will have a tough time finding a suitable match for a pretty woman like you,' I said. She went red in the face.

As we ordered desert, Shantanu walked in.

'These property sellers are tough fellows,' he said taking a seat. 'I am glad I joined Papa. Otherwise he would have been fleeced. Finally, we have a good deal.'

'Have a desert,' I suggested.

'Well I am full but I could do with some ice cream. I am sure you old friends had no dearth of subjects to talk of,' Shantanu said.

'We certainly didn't,' I replied. 'We talked of all our misdemeanours during the Ludhiana days.'

'And there was no dearth of them,' Shantanu chuckled.

Shantanu insisted on settling the bill and said he would drop me back home. We stopped by at a *Paan* shop on our way back. I had always missed a *meetha paan* after meals in Paris.

'See you soon,' Shalini said as I took leave of her and Shantanu.

The next day was heavy in terms of work. Udai had quite a few things to sort out at the income tax office – something he did not relish, he said, but had to put up with. What he dreaded the most was the complexity of income tax rules and regulations and their lending themselves to different interpretations that made life extremely difficult. And, of course, such rules were fully exploited by the tax officials to fill their personal coffers. Udai said he would need to be at the income tax office practically the whole day and asked me to go early to the factory because an important consignment needed to be dispatched the same evening. I was to leave for the factory at 8 am and woke up barely fifteen minutes before that. As I rushed out to the car after getting ready, I heard my mother shouting after me, 'Lalit, your breakfast!'

'Don't have time Mama. I shall eat something at the factory.'

'You won't get much there,' she said, holding a tall glass of milk in her hand.

'Mama, I shall get something from a nearby restaurant.'

'But I also need to talk to you,' she said.

'Talk about what?' I shouted back.

'About the Sachdevas.'

'Mama, don't irritate me. We met them yesterday. What is there to talk about?'

By this time, I was seated in the car and getting impatient. I started the car and left without giving my mother a chance to carry the conversation any further.

The traffic was unusually heavy and I found practically every traffic light turned red for me as if trying to tease me. I crossed a traffic light as it was turning red and was stopped by a policeman. It took me half an hour and a bribe of thirty rupees to sort things out with him.

I reached the factory an hour later than planned and got down to tying up various loose ends. Just when things seemed to be getting under control, my secretary announced the arrival of an inspector from the office of the Drug Controller. He wanted to see me immediately, she said.

'Usher him in.' My encounter with the policeman earlier in the day had taught me that such men in authority were not to be taken lightly.

The inspector, one Mr Kapoor, walked in. He looked an amiable smooth operator.

'Good morning Sir.' He was overcourteous for a man in authority!

'What can I do for you, Mr Kapoor?' I asked.

'You seem to be new to the place, Sir,' Mr Kapoor was all sugar and honey. 'I know the elder Mr Khanna very well and also Udai Sahib.'

'I am Mr Khanna's younger son.'

'So the secretary told me, Sir. I am very pleased to meet you.'

'What brings you here?'

'Well, Sir my duty brings me here, but we can talk of that later. I must first have your good masala chai which the elder Mr Khanna always offers me. May God grant him speedy recovery. I was pained to hear of his heart attack.'

I cursed myself for not having offered tea on my own to Mr Kapoor. He might have thousands of ways of harassing us, I thought. But it was encouraging to see that he was feeling quite at home. Tea and biscuits arrived, but unlike me that day, Mr Kapoor seemed to have all the time in the world. He talked of everything other than his business – weather, the bad state of roads, frequent power failures and what not. As he mentioned power failures, the power supply actually failed, putting the factory production on our generator that could run only some functions.

'You see this is what I was talking of,' the power failure had given Mr Kapoor an opportunity to be even more expansive in his small talk, as he had another cup of tea, before he got down to whatever he had come for.

'How can the country's industry prosper in the face of such power failures?' Mr Kapoor posed a public-spirited question. 'You see things can't improve unless the guys in the electricity department become less corrupt. I concede that it may not be possible to eliminate corruption altogether, but the extent of corruption in that department can put the thickest skins to shame.' Mr Kapoor was carrying on a monologue.

'I am a government servant, but even I had to shell out some money to get an electricity meter when I built my house. To be fair to them they gave me some concession for being a government servant,' Mr Kapoor laughed.

'Where is your house, Mr Kapoor?' I asked to make some contribution to the conversation out of politeness.

'Well, it's a small house in Sarvapriya Vihar, Sir. What else could a lowly paid government servant like me acquire?'

Mr Kapoor was being modest, I thought. Sarvapriya Vihar was certainly not a colony for lowly beings.

'You see honesty is seeped into my bones. As a public servant, I have no desire but to serve people like you. Now take this case of your factory. Your production licence comes to an end in the next two months. Udai Sahib had filed papers for its renewal. I have been asked to carry out an inspection of your production facilities for that purpose. In the normal course, one would have to take many drug samples and send them for tests to specialized laboratories located in various parts of the country. But that could take very long and possibly cause closure of the factory for some time. Now I can't do that to a good man like Mr Khanna. Besides I know that your manufacturing is completely above board. So I came just to say that I shall ensure that your licence is renewed well in time. We won't go into the testing formalities.'

'It's so kind of you,' I said. I was relieved that he had finally come to the point even though I did not like the general drift of what he had said on the production licence issue.

'You don't have to thank me, Sir. It's my duty to be helpful to entrepreneurs like you. It's just that I shall have to tackle some superiors in my department to get the licence renewed. Mind you, mine has been a life of utmost honesty. So I have no demands. But my superiors are demanding. God will definitely punish them. But so long as they are in their positions, you and I can't ignore them.'

'Well...' I fumbled for words.

'Don't worry, Sir. I know you are new to all this. Just convey what I have told you to your older brother. He knows my phone number and can discuss the matter with me.'

'All right,' is all I could manage to utter.

'I must leave now. I have other people to serve,' said Mr Kapoor as he got up.

'And tell Udai Sahib that it may take thirty grand or so to get through my difficult bosses,' said Mr Kapoor, almost as an afterthought as he left.

It was past eight in the evening when I reached home.

'Come, join us here,' my mother shouted from the family lounge. My parents and Shobha were watching the 8 o' clock TV news. Little Sanjiv was as usual making a nuisance of himself in a corner – tearing off bits of the day's newspaper and throwing them all around.

'Udai is still not back?' I asked.

'You know these income tax matters. He was stuck in the income tax office the whole day and is now sitting with our lawyer to prepare some tax papers,' said my mother. 'We are waiting for him to move to the dinner table. Will you have something in the meanwhile?' she asked.

'Some tea would be wonderful,' I said.

Shobha got up to get tea for me.

'Sanjiv you will get a solid thrashing from me if you don't stop tearing up those papers right away,' she shouted as she passed by Sanjiv. The brat gave her one casual look and went back to his destructive pursuit. He was encouraged in his annoying endeavour by my father's prompt admonition to Shobha not to harbour any thought of giving a smacking to Sanjiv.

'Do you know what our smart Sanjiv did today?' my mother asked looking at Sanjiv with eyes drooling with affection.

There we go again, I thought!

'He saw his mother putting on make-up in the morning and applying eye shadow. So he took coloured markers and drew a multicoloured pattern on his eyelids,' she said. My parents had a hearty laugh in unison.

'Poor Shobha must have had quite a time cleaning his eyelids,' said I.

'Well, that's normal for a mother. Don't forget what all I had to do for you and Udai when you were kids,' my mother was not going to put up with anything even implicitly critical of Sanjiv.

'You look very tired,' said my father.

'I am indeed very tired,' I answered emphasising each word. 'You see it was a heavy day at work and on top of that I had to put up with the unlawful demands of those calling themselves public servants.'

'What happened?' my father asked.

I narrated my experience with the policeman and my encounter with Mr Kapoor.

'Oh! So you had a visit from that scoundrel Kapoor,' said my father.

'You seem to know him well,' I said.

'For many years now. But let these things not bother you. You see you have had a protected existence so far. Now that you are fully into the family business, you will soon learn to deal with all these characters. For the moment, let Udai handle Kapoor,' my father didn't seem too concerned about what I had gone through.

Just then, Udai walked in.'How was your day?' my mother asked.

'Nothing unexpected. I had to shell out fifteen thousand in all to get the tax concessions that were due to us. If I didn't grease palms, the file wouldn't move for ages,' said Udai nonchalantly.

'Would you have tea or shall we move to the dinner table?' Shobha asked.

'I am famished. I wouldn't mind dinner right away,' Udai said.

'Eh, what are you upto? I haven't even read that newspaper properly,' Udai shouted seeing Sanjiv involved in his paper-tearing spree.

'Don't ask him that question. His right to tear paper has already been granted,' I said.'And may I know by whom?'

'Mama and Papa, of course. Who else?'

Udai had an amused look as he moved towards the door to leave the room to change before joining us at the dinner table.

'Wow!' I said uncovering a dish, '*Sarson saag*. I hope we also have *makki ki roti* with it.'

'We sure have *makki ki roti*. You can't have *Sarson saag* without *makki ki roti*. Today, we also have *maash dal*,' said my mother looking utterly pleased with my animated reaction to what she had cooked for dinner.

The meal was typical of what we had ever so often during winter. Both the dishes were always cooked by my mother in a laborious process involving cooking in an earthen pot, on low charcoal fire, that would go on for hours. She was critical of the changing ways of cooking such as pressure-cooking and maintained that even though it made things faster, it spoilt the taste of dishes. Knowing as I did the products of her slow cooking, I whole-heartedly agreed with her.

'And guess what I have made,' said Shobha.

'*Gajar ka halwa*?' I asked.

'You are right. But today you will have both *gajar ka halwa* and *moong dal halwa*,' said Shobha. Both were my favourite winter desserts.

'You are real gems,' I said hugging my mother who was seated next to me.

'Well, we are here to look after you as long as we can. I am getting old and Shobha will gradually get involved in affairs of her own family. So it's high time you thought of your own future,' said my mother with a mischievous smile on her lips.

'Don't you worry about me. I am going to stay on here with you and Shobha. So where is the problem?' said I.

'What I mean is that it's now time for you to get married and bring home my younger *bahu* to whom I could hand over the responsibility of looking after you,' said my mother serving me *saag* in a bowl with a huge blob of butter on top of it.

'Now come on Mama, I am not that old. Marriage can wait,' I tried to put her off as she passed on a *makki ki roti* soaked in butter to me.

'You are not a child anymore,' my mother was in no mood to give up.

'Mama what are you doing?' Udai shouted as he saw my mother serving *saag* to my father with a chunky piece of butter sitting on it.

My mother looked at Udai with a puzzled expression, not realising what he was objecting to.

'Papa you are a doctor and you should know that fatty diet is not good for you. You can't afford to take such risks and that too with your heart problem.'

'Well I didn't ask her to give me butter, but how can I refuse it when she gives it to me with so much of affection. Besides I am fine now and the cardiologist has even allowed me to go to the factory for a few hours every day. In fact I should be there tomorrow,' said my father with a disarming smile. Even though a doctor, he was not a great one for dietary precautions. He often admitted that he ate in plenty all the foods that he had been advising his patients to avoid.

'Papa, this is not a light hearted matter. You know you have to avoid foods rich in cholesterol,' Udai was angry at my father's attempt to end the matter in a joke.

'I know it's a serious matter. Unfortunately, with our changed lifestyles we can't have these tasty foods. My parents ate plenty of butter and ghee and yet kept healthy. The daily life involved much more of exercise those days. My father, who was a teacher, had to walk five miles to his school. There were no cars or any public transport. My mother worked the whole day at home looking after us, her children, and there were eight of us,' said my father handing back the butter in a spoon to my mother. He had realised that Udai was not going to let him get away with it.

'That's a strange logic. You mean you would much rather do without cars and mother would much rather have eight children just to be able to have greasy foods.' Udai was still angry.

'Now put an end to this argument. He is not taking butter anymore. Let's talk of something more pleasant,' said my mother to calm Udai down. She then turned to me and asked with a broad smile, 'How did you find Shalini?'

'She is a nice girl. What about her?'

'Isn't she nice? She is so pretty, good natured and well educated.'

'So she is. But what are you driving at?' I was getting concerned.

'Well, her parents have proposed her hand in marriage for you. Your father and I think she will make an excellent wife.

The Sachdevas are also such fine people and besides they are a wealthy family of our own standard.'

'The way I was packed off with her for a dinner, I knew there was something fishy. But I didn't know that you would move on such an important issue behind my back.' I protested.

'We had to plan a whole stratagem to get you two together for dinner,' my mother burst out laughing. 'Poor Shantanu had to coin an excuse to leave you two alone. He didn't go to his parents but had dinner at Machan at the Taj Mansingh itself.'

I was shocked and incensed. I looked at my father. He was smiling and had obviously been a party to the conspiracy. I gave Udai a complaining look and he shrugged his shoulders to disclaim any knowledge of what my parents were upto.

'Mama how could you do this to me?' I shrieked. The heavy work schedule of the day and my encounter with corrupt officials had left me irritable. My reaction was stronger than what it would normally be.

'We didn't commit a crime,' said my mother still smiling. 'Your father and I met each other only briefly before our marriage and that too at a religious ceremony at the home of a common friend and that was it.'

'Mama do you realise that times have changed and my marriage is very much my own affair and I must have a say in it.'

'O, come on. You have met Shalini and spent some time with her. You have known her much longer as a child. You agree with me that she is a nice girl. So what's your objection to getting married to her? You will not find a better match than that.'

'And what if I told you I don't like her,' I said in exasperation.

'Now don't change the argument. How could you not like a girl such as Shalini? You admitted that she is a nice girl,' my mother was clinging to a statement I had made about Shalini at the beginning of the evening before the issue of my marriage to her had been brought up. Her smile was gone and she had a pronounced frown.

'Mama that she is a nice girl doesn't mean I should marry her. After all, there are so many nice girls in this world. Does it mean I should marry all of them?'

'That's utter nonsense. I am not asking you to marry all nice girls in this world. I am asking you to marry a nice girl who is so well known to us.' My mother's face was getting red with anger.

'Mama I don't wish to get married for the time being. Period. Please don't force me into a marriage. It's just not done in this day and age.'

My mother was about to say something when my father interjected, 'Sheela you have just brought up the matter. You must give Lalit some time to reflect.'

'I don't think it's a mere need for reflection. I hope he is not into an affair like Sumitra's son. His was a love marriage and he is repenting at leisure,' said my mother.

'Sheela don't just assume things. It's only fair that Lalit is given some time to think,' said my father.

'And what do I tell the Sachdevas? They are expecting an answer from us.'

'Tell Mrs Sachdeva we will get back to them in two-three days.'

'Do what you like,' my mother finally gave up.

She sat with a sullen face through the rest of the evening. My father tried to lighten the atmosphere but without success. There was very little further talk on the table. I could hardly enjoy my favourite meal. I hated to hurt my mother, but she had left me no choice. As soon as my parents and Shobha left for their respective rooms after dinner, I pounced upon Udai, 'Couldn't you have warned me of this earlier?'

'I wish I knew what Mama and Papa were planning. They never discussed the matter with me. We genuinely had an evening out yesterday and Mama knew it,' Udai protested and then added, 'I know your dilemma. Do you want me to talk to papa?'

'No, if need be, I shall do so myself,' said I.

The next day, my mother did not talk to me even when she gave me breakfast. I had a meeting with our transporter first thing in the morning and it was eleven by the time I reached the factory. My father was sitting in the front lawn surrounded by a number of workers. He was a father figure to all of them and would take great pains to look after their welfare.

'Come and join us,' my father said when he saw me.

The workers were wishing him good health and telling him how concerned they had been about his illness. They added that Udai and I had looked after the factory very well but that my father's presence meant something very special to them. My father got very emotional and told them that for him each and every person working in the factory was a member of his family and that he was glad to be back to look after all of them. The workers soon left leaving us alone.

'Will you have some tea?' he asked pouring tea for himself from a kettle.

'No, thanks,' I said.

'Your mother was very upset last night.'

'Yes, I know.'

'Personally, I find Shalini a very pleasant girl and believe like your mother that she will make a good wife for you. But I see that you have some problem. Is it just the need to reflect a little more or something else? You can be frank with me.'

I kept quiet.

'Is it another woman?' my father asked.

I was hesitant to burden him with my problem.

'You know you can confide in me without any hesitation. Is it another woman?' he repeated his question.

I nodded in affirmation.

'Listening to you at the dinner table last night, I had a hunch that your hesitation to marry Shalini might be because of another woman in your life. In fact, Dr Petit had written to me about your visit to him in Tours along with a French girl. I thought you would yourself tell me about her in case there was anything serious between the two of you. After all, I have always been a very friendly father,' he said with a smile.

'Papa, I am sorry for not bringing up this matter with you earlier. But my desire to marry this French girl has run into a serious problem. It happened around the time you had a heart attack and I naturally didn't wish to saddle you with my predicament.'

'Silly boy, I remain the same caring father regardless of my illness. Nothing has changed. You can count on me as ever. I am not going to stop looking after my family simply because I had a heart attack.'

'I know that Papa,' I said sheepishly.

'Anyway tell me about this friend of yours. And what is the problem in your getting married to her? We must resolve it.'

I was overwhelmed with emotion as I recounted my relationship with Emilie. I had been stupid in assuming that I could no longer unburden myself on my father. He was still the same pillar of strength for the family that he had always been.

'What are the chances of her mother allowing her to come to India to be with you?' he asked when I finished describing my quandary.

'Well she is trying her best, but the odds are against her. Her mother doesn't keep too well and she is the only child.'

'Hmmm.' my father was pensive for some time and then said, 'You know my views. Your wishes should take the prime seat when it comes to your marriage. Your mother, of course, may have a different opinion. She would be keen that you marry an Indian girl. She is very particular on cultural and religious similarities when it comes to matrimonial alliances. But leave that to me. I shall persuade her in your favour. After all, she is your mother and wouldn't like to do anything that ruins your happiness. The main problem is the inability of this lady to join you here. Does she want you to stay in France to marry her?'

'No, Papa. She fully realises my responsibilities to my family. In fact, when I foolishly tried to stay on in France, she did her best to persuade me against it.'

'Well let's see how things develop. She may well find a way of coming here. In a worst case scenario, I would not mind your going to France if that's what your happiness demands.'

'Papa, I could never even imagine such a move. You need me, the family needs me and the business needs me.'

'Well, similarly, Emilie's mother needs her in France. One or the other of you will have to move to the other country. But, I am sure some solution would come about. Now leave all your worries to me and get on with your work,' said my father with a reassuring smile as he patted me on my back.

'And what about the Sachdevas?'

'What about them? I shall deal with them and your mother. Leave all this to me.'

The talk with my father had taken tons of load off my head and I got down to my work in an upbeat mood.

*

'I am awfully sorry, but you will agree with me that children must have a say in their marriage. It's after all a question of their life and their happiness.'

My father was on the phone when I reached home late in the evening.

'We are very fon l of Shalini. She is like our daughter. But Lalit wishes to wait for a few years before he gets married. It would be unreasonable of us to ask you to wait. Shalini is after all of marriageable age now.'

My father was obviously talking to Mr Sachdeva. A few more polite words and apologies and the phone conversation was over.

I went to the family lounge. My mother was sitting quietly in a corner. Udai and Shobha were sitting in another corner with their eyes transfixed on TV. Sanjeev's was the only voice heard in the room besides that of the TV announcer. He was making a nuisance of himself as usual, mimicking loudly the noise of a car engine and himself pretending to be the driver. However, today no one was paying any attention to him; neither his parents to check him nor my mother to admire his impish behaviour.

My father soon joined us.

'Sachdeva was quite nice about it. He seemed to show an understanding of our inability to accept their proposal regarding Shalini,' he said, evidently in an attempt to put my mother at ease. Amongst her many worries was the reaction of the Sachdevas once their proposal was rejected. She had apparently given them high hopes and had been certain that marriage with Shalini would be acceptable to me.

'What else could they do? They are civilised people and would not show their true feelings to you. I am sure they are very bitter about the manner in which we have rejected their proposal. Shalini is after all very accomplished by any standards,' my mother burst out.

'Mama, we can't ignore Lalit's views. Can we? It's after all his marriage that we are talking of,' said Udai, emphasising the word 'his'.

'I have never ignored his wishes. Who would be more concerned about his happiness than his mother? Shalini would have brought so much of joy to his life. And what is he giving her up for? A woman from a distant land and that too a Christian.'

'Sheela, she is a human being and besides Lalit and she like each other. What else matters?' said my father.

'She will have no knowledge of our values and traditions and no comprehension of our religion. What kind of a daughter-in-law will she make? God! Why did I have to see such days!' said my mother and started sobbing uncontrollably.

'Sheela, control yourself. Heavens haven't fallen. We must change with times. We can't reject the woman Lalit likes simply because she is from a different country and religion,' said my father in a firm tone.

'I can't change at this age. This woman may herself find it difficult to adjust to life in India. Besides, you tell me that she has problems in coming here to get married to Lalit. How long is Lalit going to wait for her?'

'I don't see why she should have problems adjusting to life here. Moreover, we can't find answers to all questions today. I am sure a solution will emerge in due course,' said my father.

'And in the meanwhile, your son will remain a bachelor,' my mother retorted.

'Mama, he is still young and doesn't necessarily have to get married right away. Let's put an end to this topic for today,' said Udai.

My mother fell silent again. There was very little talk at the dining table. She hardly ate. Her eyes were bloodshot. Everyone's attempts to cheer her up came to naught.

I was getting increasingly engrossed in the family business. My father had built a good reputation for our products and the demand was ever growing. Udai and I were continually meeting deadlines and my father gave us as much of assistance as he could with his state of health. My mother had grudgingly come to terms with my situation, although she never lost an opportunity to lecture me on the virtues of marrying a woman of my own community and religion.

It was the beginning of February and I was struggling, along with our mechanics, on a machine in the factory that had suddenly broken down.

'Phone call for you,' Udai shouted from the office. 'It's a trunk call from France,' he added as I approached the phone. Satellite communication was still not common those days and one had to follow the tedious process of booking a call through the phone exchange to talk to someone in another country. Udai left the office room discreetly.

'Hello, Lali,' I was thrilled to hear that voice.

'What's up?' I shouted in excitement.

'Good news,' said Emilie.

'What? Has your mother agreed to let you come to India?' My heart was pounding with excitement.

'No, on that, things are where they were when you left, but I am visiting India by the end of this month.' My excitement crashed but was salvaged to some extent by the news that Emilie was coming to India.

'How long will you be here?'

'I am attending a two-day seminar of medical researchers in Delhi and the organisers will take us for a short trip to Agra and Jaipur. I could then stay on for another week and was wondering if we could go together to Goa. My friends are full of praise for the place. I have written in detail to you.'

'I would love to visit Goa with you. What would be the dates?'

Emilie gave me the dates.

'Lali, I love you and can't wait to see you.'

'I love you too, Emie. Look forward to seeing you. Take care.'

I immediately called a tour operator friend.

'Can you get me a Braganza cottage for a week in Goa?'

My reference was to a cluster of cottages, owned by one Mr Braganza, near the Vagator beach in Goa. I had stayed there on a few occasions with friends and had found the place very convenient and reasonable in terms of costs. I loved visiting Goa. With 450 years of Portuguese colonial rule, it was a delightful blend of East and West. I enjoyed the lively company of Goans. A holiday in Goa was always an utterly rejuvenating experience and relaxation pure and simple.

'When do you want the cottage?'

I gave him the dates.

'And how many persons will accompany you?'

'Get me a cottage for two,' I said.

'And who would be the second person? I hope I am not being too curious.'

'You are indeed being nosy for a tour operator. Who accompanies me is none of your business. Just get me a cottage.'

'Will it be your French friend?'

'Just do your work and get lost,' I shouted.

'Okay as you wish,' my friend laughed as he hung up.

When I told my father about the planned trip to Goa, he was surprised at my sudden decision.

'Why this sudden plan?'

'Well, Papa, I haven't seen the Goa Carnival and this would be the right time to be there.'

Carnival is the three-day colourful annual festival of Goa heralding the time of Lent for the Goan Christian community.

'That's fine, but there will be lot of work at that time and I wonder if you could postpone your holiday by a few months. You can see the Carnival next year.'

'Papa, Emilie will be in India at that time and she wishes to visit Goa.'

I realised that I was not going to get past my father unless I told him the truth. Besides he was someone I could always confide in.

'I see. Has she decided to marry you?'

'Papa she is visiting India for a seminar and would like to spend a few days with me thereafter. She is yet to get her mother's nod for marrying me.'

'It's good that she is coming here. We would like to meet her. After all she is going to be a part of our family. I would like your mother also to meet her. I am sure that would put an end to the reservations she has on your marrying Emilie.'

'Papa, you are so kind,' I said, hugging my father. However, I was apprehensive about the proposed meeting between Emilie and my mother. She was very upset when she learnt of my visit with Emilie to Goa. With her conservative views, she found it difficult to accept that I was going on a holiday with a woman I was not married to and that too a woman who had spoilt her dream of my marrying a woman of her choice. But, with my father and Udai on my side, she could not veto my plans.

*

For six days after her arrival in India, Emilie was kept busy by the organisers of the seminar. I received her on arrival and was barely able to snatch a few minutes with her in the evening on each of the two days she was in Delhi. Finally, she was through with her conference and group visits to Agra and Jaipur and we were on our flight to Goa via Mumbai. The time on the flight was spent on exchanging notes about the last few months that we had stayed apart. There was so much to talk of.

We took a taxi from Goa's Dabolim airport and it was nearly seven in the evening by the time we reached Braganza's cottages. It was a cluster of eight cottages of varying sizes managed by Mr Braganza and his family. A tall and thin man in his early fifties, Braganza was an amiable figure. He was most of the time on the move in shorts and a tee shirt, looking to the comfort of his customers.

'Ah, my friend from Delhi. How are you, Sir?' He immediately recognised me.

'I am fine and how are you?'

'I am all right, Sir. Let me also extend a warm welcome to the charming lady.'

'This is Emilie. She is from Paris.'

'Bonjour, Mademoiselle. Je parle un peu de Francais.'

'Bonjour, Monsieur,' Emilie replied.

'Let me show you your cottage, Sir. It's almost dinner time, but you must freshen up before you come to the dining room. We have some good local music on today.'

Braganza always had one interesting performance or the other every evening for his guests.

'Why are you staring at me?' asked Emilie when we were alone in the cottage.

'I am starved of you.'

'Well, let's be clear about our priorities. I am famished. We must freshen up fast and go for dinner.'

'As you wish, but don't forget that I am starved of you.'

'Point well taken,' said Emilie with a naughty smile.

The dining room was nearly full by the time we reached there.

'How are you, Sir? What would you like to drink?' Mrs Braganza was as hospitable as ever.

'What do you suggest?' Emilie asked and added, 'I believe Goa has a very good local drink.'

'You bet it has and it's called Feni. It's distilled from cashew fruit or coconut palm. You could try cashew feni today. We make our own Feni. It's really good. You may find it a bit strong since you are taking it for the first time. I suggest you dilute it with Coke,' said Mrs Braganza. 'And what will you eat? I can offer you some continental dishes or Goan curries. Our curries have a special flavour because of the coconut milk used in them.'

'I would like to try a Goan curry,' said Emilie.

We ordered some fried rice and fish curry.

'I hope the curry won't be too spicy,' I warned Mrs Braganza, knowing as I did that Goans prefer very spicy curries.

'Don't worry, Sir. We adapt our curries to the taste of our European guests.'

The Goan music was enchanting. A great ambiance to be in with someone you loved. A group of boys and girls performed the traditional Goan song-cum-dance called *Mando*.

An orchestra was playing popular numbers and soon the dance floor was full of people.

Emilie and I danced late into the night.

Back to the cottage, Emilie grabbed me in a tight embrace and said, 'Don't forget, I have also been starved of you.'

It seemed an eternity before our mutual hunger was satiated.

*

My concept of a holiday in Goa was lazing around on its beautiful beaches, eating plenty of good food, drinking Feni, dancing to the local music and last but not the least cycling over long distances. Biking on the coconut tree lined Goan roads is, I believe, the best way of seeing Goa. Within an hour, one passes through many villages and towns and meets many friendly people. One can stop by at wayside shops to have local refreshment every now and then. One passes by small houses surrounded by coconut groves, many of them with their own poultry and piggery in the backyard. So we did all these things, but since this was Emilie's first visit to Goa, she was keen to see Goa's historic sites of which there are many. We visited the city of old Goa that was founded in the beginning of the 16th century and later colonised by the Portuguese as 'Rome of the East.' It is well known for its churches. We saw the 16th century Basilica of Bom Jesus, where the mortal remains of St. Francis Xavier are kept in a silver casket, the Chapel of St. Catherine, the Chapel of St. Francis Xavier and the most impressive of all the churches in Old Goa, the Se Cathedral. We visited Shri Mangesh Temple, dedicated to Lord Shiva, in Ponda. For journeys over long distances, we hired a motorcycle, a popular mode of transport in Goa, from Braganza. However, cycling around was a daily routine every afternoon.

One day, Emilie and I were sitting in a coconut grove to take rest in the course of a cycling trip. We saw a group of children, with school bags on their backs, passing by.

They were in the age group of eight to ten and were on their way back home from school. A girl amongst them had a severe physical handicap, apparently the result of polio.

Emilie waived out to the children. They walked up to us and one of them asked Emilie, 'Where are you from?'

'I am from France.'

'Good lord, you are from so far off. How did you come to India?'

'I came in an aeroplane,' Emilie and I found the innocent questions amusing.

'How long did you take to reach here?'

'It took me eight hours.'

'Eight hours! But doesn't the aeroplane fly very fast?'

'Of course it does, but as you said, France is so far off. So even an aeroplane takes eight hours to fly from France to India. Why don't all of you sit down? I'll give you some chocolates.'

The children were thrilled when Emilie gave them chocolates to eat.

'What do you study at school?'

'We study all subjects. Mathematics, science, social studies, English...,' it was the physically handicapped girl who answered this time.

'Okay, tell me what will all of you like to become when you grow up,' Emilie was thoroughly enjoying the conversation.

The children had different answers – doctor, engineer, singer, lawyer and what not. The handicapped girl looked up at the sky and said, 'I would like to fly a big plane between France and India.'

We were amazed at her spirit. She wanted to be an airline pilot, something her physical condition would not allow her to do.

'A child's fancy is like a bird,' said Emilie, 'that soars high in the sky, unhindered by the realities of this world or the limitations of one's circumstances. My father used to say that the best dreams that one has are as a child. The colours of dreams start fading as one moves on in age and comes to grips with the reality around. But he said that whatever one's age, one should not stop dreaming of good things to come even if the colours are not as bright as in one's childhood. Stop dreaming and you are dead, he would say.'

'I entirely agree with him,' I said.

'He had dreams of my brother and me doing big things in life when death took him away. Hardly did he know that one character of his dreams – my brother – would also not live very long.' Emilie had a distant look.

'What were your dreams as a child?' I asked her.

'Well, I wanted to become a big scientist and I continue to nurture that dream. I also wanted a prince charming of the fairy tales to brighten up my life.'

'And have you found a Prince Charming?' I asked.

'Don't fish for compliments all the time,' Emilie laughed. 'Of course, I have found a prince charming, but the compulsions of my life are hindering a happy end to the fairy tale.'

'I have no doubt it will be a happy ending. You should never lose hope.'

'I haven't lost hope. What I wish is that I don't have to choose between you and my mother.'

The children had finished their chocolates and looked somewhat bored with the philosophical conversation that Emilie and I had had. They got up to leave.

Emilie hugged the physically handicapped girl and said, 'You brave little girl, you will definitely fly a big plane one day.'

The girl gave Emilie a broad smile as she walked away with the other children in her laborious gait.

The last day of our stay in Goa happened to be the first day of the famous three-day carnival festival. We went to the capital city – Panaji – to see the celebrations there. It was feasting and merrymaking at its best. Thousands stood by the roadside seeing colourful floats go past, dancing with the music and eating and drinking to their hearts' content. It was a treat to see the participants in colourful costumes and elaborate masks. Similar festivities, we were told, take place all over Goa.

By the afternoon, we were exhausted, having danced since the morning at various places.

As we settled down for a coffee in a roadside cafe, I saw a palmist sitting on a low wooden platform some distance away. He was in a white *dhoti* and *kurta* and sported a long *tilak* on his forehead.

'Let's visit the palmist after finishing coffee,' I proposed.

'You know Lali, I don't believe in such things.'

'Well you don't have to believe in a palmist to go to him. You have seen so much of India. Would you not like to meet an Indian palmist?' I persisted.

'If you insist.'

The palmist's assistants were keeping his customers some distance away from him and allowing them to go to him one by one. It was some time before our turn came.

Emilie and I put our palms in front of him. He peered at them for some time and turned to Emilie, 'You have had a difficult time in recent years, but of late have found happiness in your life.'

Emilie kept silent.

'Do you wish to know anything in particular?' he asked.

'When will we get married?' I made bold to ask.

'Is that important? You have already found so much of happiness in each other,' the palmist's answer was vague.

'But do you think we will get married in the near future?' I persisted.

'Your commitment to each other is already more than a marital bond. Is a marriage all that significant?' the palmist remained vague.

'Can you tell the age up to which a person would live?' I asked, changing the topic.

'I am not a money maker. If I were one, I would seek to please everyone by telling them they would live very long.'

'Which means you can't predict a person's lifespan,' I said.

'I can, but I believe one should not get into this business. What is important is not the length of one's life but how one lives it. A short life well spent, not only amassing happiness for oneself but also distributing happiness to others, is far better than a long life spent aimlessly.'

'It's difficult to pin him down,' Emilie told me in French, signalling that it was time to take leave of him.

We spent our last evening in Goa at a Disco near Braganza's cottages. The palmist's answers had left me pensive. Why did he not give a clear answer on our getting married? The question was nagging me.

'Why are you so preoccupied?' Emilie asked, 'I bet it's what that palmist said or rather didn't say.'

I kept quiet.

'I told you I don't believe in such things and you would be silly to spoil your mood on what this fellow said. He was not specific on anything.'

'I think even his vague answers carried some meaning,' I said.

'I don't think so. And besides, he is not a practitioner of a precise science.'

The music had livened up. The disco was playing our favourite numbers. Feni was having its effect. My spirits soared. We came back from the disco past midnight, only because our flight back to Delhi was at eight the next morning.

We reached Delhi around ten. Emilie's departure back to France was the next day. Before we left for Goa, my father had insisted that Emilie stay with us on her return from Goa. My mother had not been happy with the idea and had tried to scotch it by saying that Swami Parmananda was to deliver a religious discourse to a gathering at our house the same evening. Swami Parmananda was a family friend, who had been a very successful businessman, but had left his business to his sons at the age of sixty to live the life of an ascetic in an ashram in Rishikesh. Each time he came to Delhi, my father would organise a get-together of friends for Swamiji's discourse. I loved the occasions. It was a treat to listen to Swamiji. He would lace his discourse with interesting anecdotes and amusing quips. What I admired the most was his humility. Unlike some other men of religion, he never claimed to possess any supernatural abilities or magical powers. He always presented himself as a normal human being sharing his thoughts with others and giving them a message of peace and happiness. He would often talk of fairly mundane things to make his point – things that we are all well aware of, but that we overlook in the mad rush of life or in times of distress. He was a scholar of the Bhagavad-Gita and his lectures were interspersed with the philosophy of Gita.

'Swamiji's discourse will not be more than an hour and I am sure Emilie will enjoy it,' said my father.

'There will be so many family friends around. What will you present this woman as?'

My mother persisted.

'I don't mind presenting her as Lalit's fiancée or she could be presented as a friend visiting from France. In any case, this is not a major issue.'

'You know my views on this matter. Do as you wish. There is nothing I can do if you are bent upon ruining the life of your son,' my mother had said, giving up her opposition to Emilie staying with us.

My father just smiled as he always did not to precipitate things each time my mother flew off the handle, which was not a rare occurrence. That was her nature.

Emilie received a warm welcome from everyone except for my mother when we reached home from the airport. There was an awkward silence as everyone sat down. My mother made an exit within a few seconds on some pretext. The silence was broken by little Sanjiv, who as usual started performing to the gallery. Everyone looked on at him for a few minutes till my father broke the ice.

'How do you find India?'

'O, it's fabulous. I have thoroughly enjoyed my holiday. Goa was wonderful.'

'I am glad you have enjoyed your holiday and we are so glad to meet you. Lalit, as you can imagine, has been full of you. I thought it would be a good opportunity for the family to get to know you.'

'It's so thoughtful of you. Lalit has spoken to me so often of your kind nature. I too am glad to meet all of you.'

I was hoping no one would raise the issue of our marriage as it was still shrouded in uncertainty. My father did not utter a word on it. The considerate person that he was, he seemed to have sensed our dilemma.

'Okay, what's the plan of action now?'asked Udai.

'They have just arrived. You should have thought of some plan,' said my father.

'And what makes you think I haven't. Shobha and I would like to take Emilie and Lalit to Bukhara restaurant. It serves delicious tandoori food. I hope you are not fed up of tandoori food by now,' said Udai looking at Emilie.

'O, no. Not at all. I have been having tandoori food during my visit here. It's delicious. How can anyone get fed up of it?'

'Okay then. Why don't you freshen up and we can leave in about an hour. Let's drive around to show you some landmarks of Delhi before lunch,' Udai proposed.

Swamiji's speech that day focused on the theme of happiness and sorrow. He explained in simple words how in the course of struggle of day-to-day life, we forget the bounties bestowed upon us by God. All that is good in life is taken for granted. Instead of being grateful to the Almighty for His many gifts, we often grieve over what is wrong or missing in our life. We thus weave around ourselves a web of sorrow, which in many cases is centred on trivial things and arises out of irrational impulses such as anger and jealousy. If worldly possessions and success were the sole source of happiness, there would be little joy in the life of poor people. However, one comes across many rich people full of sorrow and many poor persons who have happiness in their life despite their pitiable material condition. Swamiji said it was not his intention to justify perpetuation of poverty, but merely to say that happiness is a state of mind. Bhagavad-Gita maintains that true happiness does not arise from worldly possessions but out of selfless devotion to God and becoming one with the Supreme Being. The Divine consciousness or Atma dwells inside every human being. Even as sorrowful an event as death would be seen in a different light altogether if we remember that this Divine consciousness or Atma is imperishable. As the famous verse from Chapter II of Gita says, weapons cannot cleave it, fire cannot burn it, waters cannot make it wet and wind cannot make it dry. Death destroys only the physical body, but Atma lives on and travels from birth to birth until it is united with Parmatma or the Supreme Being and becomes free of the cycle of birth and death. It is only then that one finds true happiness. We ordinary human beings are perhaps far away from that state of bliss. However, even an ordinary person ought to remember that happiness depends to a very large degree upon how he or she looks at things and upon inner thinking and not necessarily upon worldly possessions and circumstances. Swamiji concluded by expressing the hope that his discourse would enable the listeners get rid of their needless worries and sorrows. Emilie raised her hand and said, 'Swamiji, may I pose a question?'

'Sure, you may. In fact I often wonder why people accept what I say as gospel truth and don't question my premises,' Swamiji smiled.

'Well, being a scientist, I am a staunch believer in scientific truth. There are those who would not accept anything as true unless it can be established beyond doubt scientifically. Therefore, there are those who would question the very existence of God. I would not go that far. But I have a doubt. Much of sorrow in life flows from stressful situations when we face uncertainty, for example, because of the serious illness of a loved one or a feared failure. People often pray to God in such situations. I wonder if they really pray to an omnipotent God or merely shore up their courage to face the stressful situation by appealing to their own inner strength and resolve.'

'I like such questions,' said Swamiji. 'The existence of God is an issue that can be debated endlessly and we don't seem to have time for that today. As far as I can see, you don't completely rule out the existence of God, but wish to know if a person praying in a stressful situation appeals for help to a superior being outside of him or to his own determination to face the situation in question. So, if you agree, I shall touch only upon that aspect.'

Emilie nodded in agreement.

'Let me then begin with something that Bhagavad-Gita says about worship of God. It talks of four kinds of worshippers

– those in distress, those seeking wealth, those seeking knowledge and those who worship without expecting a reward. The best worship is obviously the fourth kind. However, since we are talking of ordinary individuals, let's not reject the value of worship with an eye on rewards or in moments of stress. Coming to your question, even if you assume that a person appeals to his inner strength, it amounts to the same as his appealing to God, the Supreme Being outside of him. What you call a person's inner strength is in fact the Divine consciousness or Atma inside him that is but a part of the ultimate reality or Paramatma. I hope I make some sense.'

'I see your point if one were to assume that there is a Superior Being overseeing us all,' said Emilie.

'I am prepared to discuss that larger issue also,' said Swamiji. 'I could give you some time tomorrow.'

'Thank you very much, but I am leaving for my country tomorrow. I hope I shall have the pleasure of meeting you some other time.'

Refreshments for the gathering followed Swamiji's talk. Emilie was introduced to everyone as a family friend. Swamiji cornered her and said, 'Young lady, I like your spirit of enquiry, but you must remember that science doesn't offer all answers about our existence, at least not so far. Faith plays an important role in our lives.'

'I understand what you imply. I myself come from a family of believers. Both my parents have had deep faith in God. My faith was badly shaken by the tragedies that befell our family – the untimely death of my father and then of my younger brother. Add to that my scientific training and you will know where I am coming from. I am not a person devoid totally of faith. I don't completely rule out the existence of God, but I also ask myself if I can rule it firmly in,' said Emilie.

'I see your point,' said Swamiji. 'I wish we had more time to discuss this subject. I am glad to know that you are not completely devoid of faith. Remember that faith, even if you have an iota of it, can be of great help. It matters not which religion or God you believe in.'

'I'll hope to have a longer discussion with you when I am in India next,' said Emilie.

'I would be very glad to meet you again.'

Some of the invitees lingered on and it was fairly late in the evening by the time the last guest left. My father accompanied Swamiji for the governing body meeting of a charity organisation. No one was in a mood to have dinner and we got together in the family lounge to chitchat. My mother who had shunned Emilie throughout the day joined us there.

'These servants are such a nuisance. You explain a thing to them fifty times and they would still make a mistake,' she said.

'Relax Mama,' said Udai. 'The important thing is that the evening went off so well. Swamiji's discourse was spellbinding as usual and people were very happy with all the arrangements.'

'Swamiji is an orator par excellence. I think his strength lies in his coming down to the level of ordinary people in explaining complex issues to them in their language,' said Emilie.

'I liked your question to Swamiji and his answer,' said Udai.

'You said he was a rich businessman before he became an ascetic,' said Emilie to me.

'Yes he was a very successful man, but by the time he was sixty, he thought of giving the world something in return for the plenty that he had got from it and so he chose the life of an ascetic. He has invested a good deal of his own money in his ashram at Rishikesh and has a school and a dispensary there to provide free education and medical aid to the needy,' said I.

'Does he keep in touch with his family?' Emilie asked.

'His wife had passed away a few years before he became an ascetic. He has nothing to do with the day-to-day affairs of his family any more, but he visits his children whenever he is in Delhi and they also visit him in his ashram every now and then. In fact, while he is here this time, in a few days, he would attend the wedding of his nephew who has been in university with Lalit,' Udai answered.

Udai's reference to the wedding of a friend of mine gave my mother the break that she had been looking for to bring up the subject of my marriage.

'I don't know if you have discussed this subject during your visit to India, but I believe you two wish to get married,' she said with her gaze fixed on Emilie.

'Mama, why don't you leave this matter to us,' said I before Emilie could say anything.

'I am talking to Emilie and would ask you not to butt in,' my mother was not prepared to brook any interference.

'What have you thought of your marriage?' she again turned to Emilie.

'Well, we are both very keen to get married as soon as possible, but I need to resolve a problem I have,' said Emilie.

'And what is that problem?'

'Mama, you know the problem very well...' Udai tried to interrupt her this time.

'I wish to hear it from Emilie,' said my mother emphasising the word 'wish' and added, 'Why don't you allow her to talk? Don't you realise you are being rude to a guest?'

'Let me explain the problem,' said Emilie. 'You may know that I am the only surviving child of my mother who is not keeping good health. I therefore find it difficult to leave her alone in France to join Lalit here.'

'How do you propose to resolve this problem?' my mother persisted.

'Well...' Emilie was at a loss for words.

'The fact is you may not be able to find a solution to your problem. Health deteriorates and does not improve as one gets on in years. What would you do if your mother continues to have health problems?'

'Mama, such things need some time to resolve. You can't find solutions overnight,' said I in a prickly tone.

'I am not talking of an overnight solution. What I am saying is that there may be no solution to this problem.' My mother then turned to Emilie and added, 'Look, all that I want you and Lalit to do is to face the reality and not live in a make-believe world. I wonder if a marriage between people such as you, with vast cultural and religious differences, is such a great idea. I am told that I am old fashioned and need to change with times. So I am not labouring that issue. But your problem in leaving France seems to me to be intractable.'

'Lalit and I love each other and I am sure a solution would come about,' said Emilie.

'How?' my mother almost shrieked, 'Don't you think you are holding my son back from getting on with his life?'

'Mama, this is too much...'I shouted. Udai's face was red with anger.

'Let me talk,' said Emilie in a firm tone. She was also losing her patience.

She turned to my mother and said, 'I am not holding back your son from doing anything. If he is waiting for me to resolve my problem, it's because he loves me as much as I love him.'

'Yes, but the difference is that while he is ready to marry you, in your case there is a difficulty that is not likely to go away. Don't you think you are ruining the life of my son? But for you, he would soon be happily married to a good Indian woman,' my mother was hysterical by now.

'This has gone too far,' Udai shouted.

Before my mother could say anything further, Shobha gently persuaded her to leave the room.

'I am awfully sorry,' said Udai to Emilie. 'She has a quick temper and very often says things without really meaning them. Please don't mind what she said. The family is very much with your and Lalit's decision to get married.'

'No, I don't mind what she said. It's natural for her as a mother to be concerned about Lalit's future,' said Emilie with a faint smile.

A heavy silence hung in the room for a few seconds and was broken by Emilie, 'I better get going with my packing. I have an early start tomorrow morning.' She left for the guest room.

'I am so sorry for what has happened. I can understand your feelings,' said Udai, putting his hand on my shoulder. I said nothing.

'I think we too should call it a day. It's fairly late,' Udai changed the topic.

'Let's wait for father to come back,' said I, hoping to linger on in Udai's company for some more time. I dreaded being alone after the evening's unpleasant argument and knew that it would not be easy to get sleep. I also had a sub-conscious desire to apprise my father of what had transpired in the hope that as always he would calm down my ruffled sentiments.

I had barely finished my sentence when the doorbell rang and it was father. He looked pale in the face and slightly breathless.

'Are you all right?' Udai asked.

'I am a little tired,' said father sitting in a chair.

'You look so pale. I better call Dr Ahuja,' said Udai.

'Let's wait for some time. I should be fine,' father insisted.

The chauffeur who had brought him back said that he had been fine when he left the meeting of the charity organisation but had started feeling slightly uneasy on the way.

Udai and the chauffeur helped father to his bed and I rang up our family physician Dr Ahuja. Mother started sobbing seeing father in that state. The resulting commotion brought Shobha and Emilie also out of their rooms.

Dr Ahuja was in within a few minutes.

'You look all right Khanna Sahib. Don't worry; we will sort out any minor problem that you may have,' he reassured my father with a smile as he got down to his check up.

He took an ECG, peered at the graph and said much to the relief of everyone, 'There is nothing to worry. It seems to be a case of exhaustion. I believe you had a rather long day. I have cautioned you repeatedly to take it easy. Udai tells me that you also remain overactive at the factory. When I allowed you to resume visits to the factory, it was with a clear caveat that you would not strain yourself too much. And why should you – the father of two grown-up sons – exert yourself on business matters.'

'Well, I am not going to argue with you. I know that being a doctor; it's your right to lecture me to take it easy and it's my right to get on with my life as best as I can,' said father with a disarming smile.

'Don't forget I have your family on my side. They will ensure that my instructions are carried out. Anyway, you should take complete rest for three days. Right now I shall give you a tranquilliser so that you could sleep well.'

Dr Ahuja gave father an injection and it was well past midnight by the time everyone retired for the night. I could sleep only in fits and starts and was up at six the next morning as I was to accompany Emilie to the airport. Udai and Shobha saw her off from the house. She regretted not being able to say goodbye to my father, as he was still asleep.

There was complete silence in the car as Emilie and I hit the road for the airport. There was very little traffic at that time. Last night's tense discussion was still very much on our minds.

'Hope you enjoyed your stay in India,' I said to lighten the atmosphere a little.

'O, it has been wonderful,' said Emilie and a heavy silence ensued.

'You know I shall miss you every second and shall wait eagerly for the day when we can be together in marriage,' said I.

'I shall miss you too. It's a terrible feeling not to know when I may be able to join you.'

'I am sure we will soon be together.'

'Do you really think so?' said Emilie trying to catch my gaze as I avoided hers.

'Have faith in God. He brought us together and He will show us a way out of our dilemma,' I tried to reassure her.

'I really don't know who brought us together. God or chance. If it was God, I wonder if He cares for human emotions. If, on the other hand, it was chance, it would be too much to expect it to be conscious of human feelings.'

'My father would be willing to let me migrate to France if nothing else works out.'

'You know I have never favoured such a move. And did you hear what his doctor had to say yesterday?'

'Don't despair. This is not the time to think of such complex issues. We are both tired. We will continue to apply our minds and I am sure a solution would come about.'

'I don't know how. Sometimes our respective situations look like two parallel lines that may never meet.'

'Emilie, have faith at the very least in our love.'

'That's what has sustained me so far.'

There was nothing further to say. Silence followed again.

We were soon at the airport. I waited for a few minutes till Emilie crossed over to the restricted area, waiving to me with a fleeting smile. My head was a jumble of emotions and confusion when I drove back home.

Life went back to its routine after Emilie's departure. Weekly letters came from her giving her news. Each time she sounded more despondent than before. Mme Martin's health was causing increasing concern and she was back with Emilie in Paris. The pressure of looking after Mme Martin and her work was proving to be too much for Emilie. After about two months, I got a short letter saying Mme Martin had suffered a stroke and was hospitalised. For the next six weeks, I received only two letters just to say that Mme Martin's condition continued to be bad and Emilie would write a longer letter as soon as she could. And then I did get a longer letter, but one that I wished had never arrived. It was written in a melancholic tone and completely shattered me. Each word came flying like an arrow, piercing my flesh and causing unbearable pain. 'I am writing this letter with a heavy heart and after a great deal of deliberation,' Emilie had written, 'Barely two years ago, I did not know you at all. And then you came in my life and I found the man of my dreams. My love for you has known no bounds. Even though we are separated by a long distance, the very thought that you are mine has comforted me all along and given me a sense of security, especially at a juncture when my life has been full of problems. But precisely because I love you so much, I must not do anything that hurts you. I would be very selfish if I were to keep you tied up in a relationship whose future grows more uncertain with each passing day. Our respective lives look increasingly like two parallel lines that are not destined to meet. My mother is back home, but she is badly crippled. Her doctor is unable to say if she will recover and if so, in how much time. He cannot say how long she will live. She is completely dependent on me. Even if I shift her to an old peoples' home – something I may be obliged to do eventually if I have to continue to earn my living – I can't come to India leaving her back here. I have never favoured your leaving your family to join me here. Besides, your family needs you, the family business needs you and above all, your father needs you. I would hate to do something that causes pain to an angel like him. I have stayed awake for the last several nights thinking on this issue. I have often cried at my inability to give you the happiness that you so richly deserve. I am convinced that I am keeping you away from a happy future that awaits you if you marry a good Indian woman. I know what I am going to say will hurt you a great deal, but feel it will be in your long term interest. I believe the time has come for us to put an end to our relationship. I don't know what is to become of my life, but I hope you will not carry the burden of my woes on yourself and will get on with your life. The year and a half we have known each other has been the loveliest part of my life and I am sure of yours too. So long as we are alive, it cannot die. I hope that with passage of time, it will recede into some corner of our consciousness, perhaps to come alive and torment us every now and then. But, that would be better than my ruining your future by clinging to a bond whose obligations I cannot fulfil. I have taken leave from my place of work and we will be moving out of Paris in the next few days. I shall try to get a lighter job in a smaller city where I can count on the help of our relations and devote some time to my mother. I would request you not to write to me or try to get in touch with me anymore. That would only prolong our agony. You should know that I shall always pray for your success and happiness. It was so nice knowing you and I don't think I shall ever find the happiness that I found in you. But then maybe I was not destined to keep it. I hesitate to close this letter with "Au revoir" because I would not like to come back in your life to ruin the happiness that I am sure you will find. Be happy wherever you are.'

My world came crashing around me. I was angry and confused as I read the letter again. How could Emilie do this to me? How could she imagine that I would just forget her? If love were that easy to wish away, we would have done so when I came back to India. My head was throbbing with pain. I wanted to do something to put my crumbling world together again. But, what could I do? As the contents of Emilie's letter started sinking in, I picked up the phone and booked a call to her residence number. It was seven in the morning in France, but no one answered her phone. Later in the day, I called her place of work. They said she had gone out of Paris. They did not think she would come back to work with them. They had her new address, but she had barred them from giving it to anyone without her consent. If I wrote to her at their address, they would forward my letter to her. I wrote a long letter expressing my shock, bewilderment and anger and pleading with Emilie not to take a hasty decision. As I had finished writing the letter, Udai stepped into the factory office. He had been out to our lawyer that morning.

'Why are your eyes so red?' he asked.

I told him about Emilie's letter.

'I am awfully sorry, but I could see it coming. She is right in saying that your relationship may keep not only your but also her future hostage without any certainty of your getting together anytime soon. I can imagine your pain. Let's hope she reconsiders her decision.'

I told Udai I was not feeling well and would go home to take some rest. My father was home when I reached there. I told him I had a severe headache and went to my bedroom to lie down. As I lay in bed, painful thoughts kept racing through my mind. I heard my father's footsteps approaching my room.

'What is wrong with you, Lalit?' he asked, 'You were perfectly fine this morning.'

'I seem to have a cold, Papa.'

'Would you like to take some medicine?'

'No, I should be fine by tomorrow.'

'Have you heard from Emilie of late?' My father was a very perceptive person and had an uncanny sense that told him that my problem was not connected to a cold.

'I got a letter from her this morning,' I found an opportunity to unburden myself on the person who I was sure would give me the comfort that I badly needed.

'Hope she is fine. You had mentioned to me that her mother had been unwell. How is she now?'

'She is seriously crippled.'

'I am very sorry to know that. Must be hard on poor Emilie.'

'She is finding it difficult to combine her job with looking after her mother and is planning to take up a lighter job in a smaller city where they could get the help of some relations.'

'That's a sensible thing to do. But let it not bother you. These are phases in life everyone goes through. I am sure her mother will recover soon.'

'I hope so too, but burdened by the current state of affairs, Emilie has taken a shocking decision to end her relationship with me.'

'Hmmm, I knew from your demeanour that something was terribly wrong,' father said without showing any sign of anxiety. He had the ability to take the most shocking bits of news without losing his cool. However, he had become pensive.

'And why has she taken this decision?'

'She believes she is keeping me tied up in a relationship which has no chance of coming to fruition anytime soon because of her problems and she would therefore like to leave me to get on with my life.'

'The poor girl seems to be under too much of stress and does not know what she is doing. Give her some time to get out of the current mess and she should be able to see things differently. Why don't you speak to her on phone?'

'I tried but she is not available at her residence or office. She has already left Paris and has asked her office not to give her new address to anyone without her authorisation. I have written a letter to her at her office address and they have promised to forward it to her new address.'

'Good, I am sure you will get a reply revising her decision when she looks at things a little more coolly. You must give her some time to clear out the confusion in her head.'

'I hope she changes her decision.'

'I am sure she will. Now get up and let's go to the market. I have to buy some books and a new pair of shoes. Lying around alone here is not going to help.'

Emilie's letter still weighed heavy on my head, but my father had as usual given me the psychological comfort that I was badly in need of. We were soon sitting in a cafeteria in the market and I was feeling much better.

*

I never got a reply from Emilie. My efforts to find her new address were in vain. Her office in Paris said they had forwarded my letters to her. After a few months, they told me that she had shifted from the address that she had given them and that since they had no further dealings with her, they had not obtained her latest address. Catherine had left her job in Hilton and had apparently gone on a long world tour. As for Sunil, I had got a letter from him within a few weeks of my return to India saying he and Brigitte were going to Sri Lanka as he had failed to get a job in France and that he would be in touch. I had not heard from him thereafter. During one of my subsequent visits to France for work at Remedes, I went down to Poitiers only to find that Mme Martin's house had been sold and the new owners did not know where the former owners had gone.

Shock and anger had driven me crazy. My father slowly managed to get me out of that frame of mind. Initially, he told me ever so often that it was a matter of time before Emilie changed her decision. However, as time went by and the hope of Emilie getting back to me faded, he consoled me by saying that time was the greatest healer and that things would look up again. Soon after she got to know of Emilie's decision, my mother started pestering me to get married and said she was looking around for a suitable match. She realised quickly enough that I was not going to give in. About a year after Emilie cut off all links with me and when all attempts to get in touch with her had failed, my father gently told me to consider getting married.

'Marriage and your own family will help you forget the misfortune you have been through,' he said.

'Papa, I have no intention of getting married. I dread building another relationship,' I was emphatic.

'Not every relationship is destined to end the same way. You have a long life to live. Your mother and I will not be around forever. Udai will also get more and more involved in his own family. You must look to your own future. It would be very difficult to live your life all by yourself.'

'Papa, you told me that time is the greatest healer and now that traumatic memories have just about started to fade, please don't revive them by bringing up this subject.' Thereafter, my family tried several times to persuade me to get married, but in the next year or two, they realised that my determination was firm and gave up. As my days with Emilie slowly retreated to an unknown corner of my mind, I built up a new life for myself. The factory took a lot of my time. In my spare time I played a lot of golf. Over the weekends, I spent some time at an orphanage that Swami Parmananda's family had set up. I, along with other volunteers, organised sports and other leisure activities for children. These were children often from very poor families and had gone through extremely tragic circumstances. However, they had started a new life and I never found them brooding over their past. Some were too young to know about their adversity. Others, who were old enough to have unpleasant memories, were also rarely glum. They all greeted me with a broad smile each time I visited them. They gave me so much of love in return for the little time I gave them. In their smiling faces, I saw an eternal hope and the capacity of life to look up even after the most trying times. Soon my new lifestyle formed a cocoon around me and I began to live in its emotional safety. It was this cocoon that had been breached by Emilie's coming into my life again.

The memory lane had suddenly come to a dead end. It was as if I had recalled a life that had been destroyed in one brutal stroke and that had, therefore, left nothing to recall beyond the moment it came to an end. I looked at my watch. It was two in the morning. I was astonished at the vividness of all the memories of my days with Emilie after so many years during which I had consciously resisted reviving them. The appearance of a dead end was unnerving. 'Why did it have to end this way?' The question had cropped up in my mind yet again years after I had stopped asking it. There was no sign of sleep. The room had become overheated. I rolled up the window shutter and opened it a little. The neon sign across the window was flashing intermittently. I sat on a chair, my eyes transfixed on the sign. The light came on one moment, dazzling bright, and then died out the next, but only to come on dazzling bright once again. I kept staring at it – bright and completely dark and then the whole cycle repeating itself again – and slept in the chair itself in fits and starts.

The phone ring woke me up. It was Claude calling from his home.

'Listen, I may be a little late in coming to office today. I am afraid we will have to postpone our 9.30 appointment by an hour if that's all right by you. I shall inform Maitre Bernard also.'

I looked at my watch. It was already 8.30 and in any case I wouldn't be able to keep to the 9.30 appointment.

'That's fine by me, Claude.'

It was fortunately a sunny, though cold, day. A bright day can make all the difference when one is going through a hard time. Having relived my days with Emilie the previous night, I had a strong urge to see her. I got ready and went to Café de Nice.

'Bonjour, Monsieur Khanna.' Pierre had a smiling face as ever. 'Please make yourself comfortable. I shall be with you in a minute.'

He was back shortly.

'What will you have?'

'Get me the strongest coffee you have ever made,' said I with a smile.

'Hope all is well, Monsieur.'

'It's just that I had a sleepless night and have a good deal of work today. So I must keep awake.'

'Don't worry, Monsieur. My coffee will ensure that you keep awake for the next three days,' Pierre didn't regard modesty as a virtue.

'Now don't overdo it. I need to keep awake only through the day and must sleep tonight if I have to keep fit.'

'Very well Monsieur, I shall ensure that my coffee keeps you awake precisely for twelve hours from now. If you feel too bright by the time you come to me for dinner, I shall give you another drink to neutralise any excess caffeine,' Pierre chuckled.

'God bless you for inventing such precision effect drinks. Also give me two croissants with some butter and jam.'

'Get Monsieur two croissants with butter and jam,' Pierre shouted to Anne. 'And I shall make my magical coffee for him myself.'

Pierre was not only a good café owner; he was also a great friend for all his customers. His cheerful and jovial disposition was so welcome first thing in the morning.

Breakfast over, I walked up to the nearest Metro station and took a metro to Porte de Saint Cloud from where I would take one to Boulogne.

'Bonjour Monsieur Khanna. Claude and Maitre Bernard are already waiting for you. Today they beat you to it,' Mireille giggled.

We had covered a large part of the agreements for negotiations the previous day and I hoped that it would be a relatively easy day today. But that was asking for too much when you were up against Maitre Bernard. He brought up a number of new clauses that he said had been missed out the previous day. Most of these related to a situation flowing from the inability of either of the parties to perform the contract because of natural and manmade disasters.

'Why must you think of such horrible things,' Claude and I protested.

'A good lawyer must take care of all contingencies if he is to ensure the long term peace of mind of his clients,' said Bernard in all seriousness. He then embarked upon what threatened to be a long lecture on the manner in which disasters could strike all of a sudden without any warning and the consequent need to provide adequately for them. The lecture had the potential of ruining our peace of mind much before the disasters actually struck, if at all they struck. Therefore, Claude and I made an immediate surrender by agreeing to go over all the clauses in question, thereby cutting short Bernard's disastrous discourse. Our negotiations took the best part of the day and it was decided that we would go to Bernard's office the next day to have a look at the final text and sign the agreements.

'Good work. I am glad we are through with these negotiations. Finalising such agreements is the most tedious part of my work. I wish we could just work on trust on each other, but then Maitre Bernard thinks otherwise and perhaps he is right,' said Claude.

'We may have to work on another agreement,' said I.

'Now what is that?' Claude asked with a wrinkled forehead.

'You remember your offer of the preparation for hypertension. Udai called me yesterday to say that the necessary clearances on the Indian side have been obtained and he would like me to finalise and sign an agreement on that drug too while I am here. He also wants me to familiarise myself with its production line.'

'That's great news even though it means working on yet another agreement.' Claude was a good salesman and movement on a new business opportunity would not fail to please him.

'Well we can work on the agreement in the coming days, but when can I start going to the factory to spend time on the production line?' I asked.

'You can start doing that tomorrow, but I hope you realise that Christmas and New Year holidays would fall in between and that may mean a longer stay for you spilling into January.'

'I mentioned that to Udai and he doesn't mind my staying on a little longer.'

'Good, we too would love to have you with us for a longer time.'

'I hope I'll not be required to put in very long hours at the factory.'

'You could start at nine every morning and call it a day at about three in the afternoon,' said Claude.

'That would be perfectly fine,' said I.

We finished for the day at four. Bernard left immediately as he was to see another client. Claude stepped out to see his director general. I was left alone. I suddenly remembered that I was wearing the same suit that I had worn the day before, during my journey from London to Paris. I rummaged through the coat pocket and fished out Sunil's visiting card with Emilie's number at its back. I dialled the number. The phone kept ringing without any answer. I tried after a few minutes and there was still no response. I stepped out and met Claude in the corridor. He said he had already informed the production in-charge at the factory, who would be expecting me at ten the next day.

Café the Nice was as crowded as ever when I reached there for dinner. I went straight to their phone and dialled Emilie's number once again. Still no response. I was getting impatient. To meet Emilie. To see once again that beautiful face that had suddenly disappeared from my life. To hear that voice that was so dear to me. To see her just once. And then a doubt. How would she react to my getting in touch with her? She would certainly have a family of her own and might not like my barging into her life, uninvited, after such a long time. But then the doubt was drowned by my burning desire to see her. I called Sunil to ask if he had Emilie's address. He said Brigitte might have it but she was out with some friends. He would call me first thing in the morning the next day in case she had it. He called the next day to give me the address.

Claude and I visited Maitre Bernard's office to give finishing touches to our agreements and I spent some time at the Remedes factory. At 3 pm I went to Emilie's apartment block. The entrance door of the building was locked and I did not have the access code. After some time, a woman came to the entrance lobby and opened the door for me. I gave her Emilie's apartment number and she said that it had remained locked for the last two days that she had been there to stand in for her husband who was the caretaker of the building and was on leave for a few days.

'Would you know where the residents of that apartment are?' I asked.

'I don't, but my husband might know,' she said.

'Could you please find it out for me?' I pleaded.

The woman went into a room on one side of the lobby saying she would try to get in touch with her husband on phone.

She emerged after some time to say that the occupant of the apartment was sick and admitted in hospital Pitier-Salpetriere.

'Anyone from her family around?' I asked.

'I didn't ask my husband about her family, but I haven't seen anyone in that apartment during the two days I have been here.'

I thanked the lady and asked if I could make a phone call. She led me into the caretaker's office. I called the Pitier-Salpetriere hospital and told the operator that I was looking for an indoor patient. She put me through to the enquiry. I asked the lady at the other end if they had an indoor patient named Emilie.

'What is her family name?' the lady enquired.

'Well, it is Martin,' I said hesitatingly, not knowing what family name Emilie had in case she was married.

'Ah, yes. She is here in ward number seven.'

'Many thanks. What are your visiting hours?' I asked.

'You can visit her till five today.'

It was already past three thirty. If I rushed, I might be able to make it before five. Upon my request, the lady gave me the name of the metro station near the hospital. The metro journey to the hospital was an agonising wait before I met Emilie. It was also an anxious time. Why was she in hospital? I hoped it was nothing serious.

It was around four thirty that I reached the hospital in the 13th district. As I walked upto the reception, I noticed that my apprehension had given way to boundless excitement at the prospect of meeting Emilie again. The fact of her illness had receded from my mind. Instead I was curious about how she would react on seeing me after such a long time and that too completely unexpectedly. The receptionist guided me to the ward where Emilie was admitted. As I approached the nurses' station, a plump elderly nurse enquired if she could be of any help. On being informed of the purpose of my visit, she pointed out

Emilie's room while saying, 'You must hurry up. The visiting hours come to a close in another twenty minutes.'

Giving a gentle knock on the door, I entered the room. Emilie was alone and fast asleep. The disease, whatever it was, had reduced her body to a near skeleton. Her cheeks were sunken and pale. A grey tinge had marred the beauty of her lips. A scarf was tied around her head, covering her auburn hair. The surface of the scarf did not reveal any bulges underneath. Perhaps her hair was no more. I stood still, traumatised by her state.

The plump nurse walked in and said in a loud tone, as if making a public pronouncement, 'Time to take your temperature, my dear.'

Emilie stirred a little. The nurse was blocking her view of where I was standing. Having taken the temperature, she moved to the other side of the bed to record it on a chart. Emilie's eyes caught sight of me. She had a puzzled expression on her face for a few seconds. Then her lips broke into a faint smile. They quivered as she said something that was inaudible, but the movement of her lips told me that she had tried to utter my name – Lali, as she used to call me. Emilie's smile failed to light up her eyes as it used to in good old days. Life seemed to have been drained out of them. She kept peering at me for the next few seconds until the nurse's voice rang out again, 'Well, dear Emilie, all is well. I'll get your dinner in half an hour.'

The nurse's words of reassurance seemed to have little impact on Emilie. She made a week gesture with her hand to say that she did not feel like eating anything.

'You must try to eat, even if a small quantity. I shall be back shortly,' the nurse said, patting Emilie's forehead. As she moved towards the door to leave, she turned back to say, 'I am afraid, Monsieur, you will have to leave in a few minutes.'

'I shall do so, Mademoiselle.'

I walked upto Emilie. She again smiled as I held her hand. She looked utterly exhausted and shut her eyes.

'How are you?' I asked.

'Not too well,' she said in a barely audible tone and fell silent. I realised that she was not in a position to talk much. I stood there silently, holding her hand. It was already a few seconds past five.

'I must leave now,' I finally said.

'Will you come again?' I heard a feeble voice.

A lump rose in my throat. I suppressed it to say, 'Yes, of course. I will. I am here for a few weeks.'

When I reached the reception, I saw a familiar figure. It took me a few seconds to realise that it was Catherine. She had changed a great deal – had greyed and put on 'weight.

'Hello, Catherine, do you recognise me?'

'Aren't you Lalit? What a surprise!'

'I came to know of Emilie and was here to see her. She seems to be in a bad shape.'

'She indeed is. It's cancer. I too was with her until half an hour ago and then spent some time in sorting out the settlement of her treatment bills.'

'What do the doctors say?' I asked.

'It's bad,' said Catherine and added, 'Look, I must rush back home. We are expecting some guests and are taking them out for dinner. Call me and we can talk more.'

She scribbled her phone number on a piece of paper and rushed out.

I tried to call her later in the evening but the phone kept ringing. I was still not fully aware of the stage of Emilie's illness expect for the fact that her physical state was hardly encouraging.

*

I spent the better part of the next day at the Remedes factory. I again tried to call Catherine but no one answered. It was her home number and no one seemed to be there. Having finished the day's work, I made my way to the hospital. Visitors' hour had just commenced when I stepped into Emilie's room. She seemed more alert than the previous day, welcomed me with a smile and made a gesture asking me to take the chair by her bedside. Within a few minutes, the plump nurse came with a medicine. She seemed less forbidding than the previous day, perhaps because I was meeting her the second time. While she was still there, a senior doctor, accompanied by his juniors, walked in.

'How are you?' the doctor enquired.

'I am feeling somewhat better today,' Emilie said in a frail voice.

'I can see you look better than yesterday. In fact each day that you move away from the recent course of chemotherapy, you will feel better still. In a few days, we will make an assessment on how effective this round of chemotherapy has been.'

'What if it has not been effective?' Emilie asked.

'We will cross that bridge if and when we come to it. I would not rush to any judgment,' the doctor said.

'What if it is not effective?' Emilie persisted. 'I need to know. You have always been forthright with me and I hope you will answer my question frankly'.

'Well I am afraid in that case we will not be left with very many options.'

Emilie shut her eyes and took a deep breath, as if trying to absorb the shock of the doctor's statement.

'But I must emphasise that we are today not at that stage. I must make an assessment in a few days and only then can I say something more definite. Let's not rush to any conclusions,' said the doctor.

Emilie nodded.

'Now you must slowly recover your strength. I know chemotherapy has been very harsh on you. I shall see you again tomorrow.' The doctor and his retinue departed.

Emilie looked at me and gestured to me to move my chair a little closer to her bed.

'He is Dr Jacques Beaujean, in-charge of my treatment. A very fine person,' she said.

'How long have you had this problem?'

'About three years now. It started as breast cancer. I was operated upon and was fine for over a year. Then it invaded my lungs necessitating the first round of chemotherapy that gave me relief. It has now invaded my lungs again and has been spreading very fast. I have gone through yet another round of chemotherapy and you heard what the doctor said.'

'I think he was right in saying that it may be premature to rush to any conclusions. I am sure you will recover soon.'

'I hope so too. I am tired of being bedridden for long spells. But things don't look too bright this time around.'

'I can see that you have gone through a difficult time, but there is no need to despair. Don't forget the doctor's advice not to draw any hasty inferences.'

Emilie nodded.

There was sudden silence in the room. Emilie's gaze met mine and she looked away. Was she trying to avoid my gaze? Were the thoughts going through my mind going through hers too? All that she had summed up for me was her illness over the last three years. She had so much else to explain. What had happened when she suddenly cut off all links with me? Why did she do it? Was this an appropriate occasion to pose all those questions to her? She was already physically and mentally utterly worn out. Reviving our difficult past may cause her greater stress. Much as I was dying to get answers to the questions that were tormenting me, I could not muster the courage to pose them. Emilie had shut her eyes and was breathing gently. My gaze fell on her face. I remembered her lively face smiling in front of me, her blue eyes absorbing all the beauty of the world, her arms taking me in a blissful embrace, her lips kissing me passionately and her infinite energy ready to conquer the world. Where was that Emilie? Why was she suffering so much? Why had she wasted away in such a cruel manner?

Emilie opened her eyes.

'How have you been?' she asked.

She had broached the subject I had been hesitant to address.

'I have been fine,' I answered.

'Your family?'

'My parents passed away a few years ago. Udai and his wife are fine. They have a son – Sanjeev whom you had seen during your visit to India – and a daughter who was born later on.'

'And your own family?'

'That's my family. I live with Udai and his family in the same house where you had visited us.'

Emilie looked away and there was heavy silence again. This time I broke it, 'How have you been?'

'I have been all right except for this illness for the last three years. My mother passed away within five-six years of our parting ways.'

The word 'our' cut me to the quick. Parting ways had not been my decision. I had been given no option. I tried to suppress my hurt and not say anything that would cause anguish to Emilie, but before I knew, my mouth blurted out, 'Our parting ways?'- emphasising the word 'our'.

'I am sorry for using the word 'our'. I know it was not your decision. But I was under so much of stress. I was not free to take a decision about my future and it seemed I might remain in that state forever. I didn't want to ruin your future and keep you tied down to my misfortune.'

'I wish you had left it to me to judge what would or would not ruin my future.'

'I know I caused you a deep hurt, but I realised it much later. I was not in a proper state of mind when I took the decision to part ways. At that stage it seemed I was taking a decision in your best interest. I knew it would shatter you in the short run, but I thought it would be good for you in the long run.'

'Why didn't you get in touch with me when you realised that you had not been fair to our relationship?' I was trying my best to resist an argument, but my pent up anguish was flowing over.

'I thought it might be too late, you might have moved on with your life and I might re-enter it only to cause you further grief.'

'What made you think I could move on in my 1ife without you? I wish you had realised that our relationship involved two persons and it was unfair of one to take unilateral decisions.'

'I know I have been very unfair to you. I wish I could seize that moment when I made a horrible decision and correct it. All that I can do now is to apologise to you for the terrible wrong I did to you. You didn't deserve it.'

'You know how much I loved you. Over the years I thought I had put your memory in some unknown corner of my mind, but I now realise how wrong I was. Nothing seems to have changed between us as far as I am concerned. Nothing that you would ever do to me would deserve an apology. In my eyes, you are still my perfect Emilie who can do no wrong.'

Emilie was sobbing. Her breathing had become laboured. I held her hand and gently stroked her forehead. I felt wretched for having made her cry. I was also tormented by the thought that I might have erred in expressing my unchanged feelings for her. What if she had moved on in her life?

Emilie's breathing eased slowly. She lay before me, utterly fatigued, her eyes shut.

The visitors' hour was coming to an end.

'Emilie,' I whispered.

She opened her eyes.

'I have to leave now. The visitors' hour has come to an end. I shall visit you again tomorrow.'

'It's so nice to have you here.'

'It's so nice to see you after such a long time.'

She smiled. I gently kissed her hand before I left.

With Christmas approaching in a few weeks, the streets of Paris wore a festive look with colourful decorative lights all around. Champs Elysees looked absolutely gorgeous as I made my way towards my hotel. I was weighed down by the desperation of Emilie's situation and feeling very restless. Whenever I was in a similar state in India, I would go to the temple close to our home and spend some time there to regain my peace of mind. I didn't know of any temple in Paris. So I decided to go to the Notre Dame church. In any case, my God had never been confined in the narrow bounds of any particular religion. My father had often told me that all roads led to Him and what was important was faith in Him. I sat in the church looking at the altar.

'Please do something to help Emie,' I prayed. 'Don't let such a promising and vibrant life come to such an abrupt end.'

'Please help Emie,' I repeatedly uttered in my heart over the next few minutes as peace slowly descended on me. 'God will do something to help her,' a voice within me said. What exactly? I did not know. But the thought that He would do something put an end to the agitation in my mind. It was nearly an hour later that I walked out of the church and made my way to Café de Nice. The place was crowded as usual, but Pierre quickly found me a place.

'Hope all is well. You look a little preoccupied,' said Pierre.

'Well, I am a little agitated at the moment.'

'And what is it? Can I help in any way?'

'It's a lady I had known here and loved madly long ago. She is suffering from cancer and the doctor says they could soon run out of options.'

'Hmmm, I can appreciate your feelings, but medicine these days can work wonders and let's not think options have run out until they really run out,' Pierre tried to encourage me.

'That's what the doctor says. He believes it may be premature to jump to any definite conclusion for the moment.'

'There you are,' said Pierre, 'now relax and have a nice meal.' He rattled off his proposals for the dinner and took my order.

'You know you can talk to me anytime you feel burdened by this problem,' said Pierre. He was as ever good as gold. I indeed needed to talk to someone about Emie. My conversation with her had given me some idea of her disease and why she had decided to break off with me. But I still did not know all that I wanted to know. What about *her* family? Who was looking after her? What had she done with *her* life after breaking off with me? I used Pierre's phone to call Catherine.

'Listen, I need to talk to you about Emilie. I was with her earlier today and from what the doctor said, her situation seems pretty bad,' said I.

'I told you she is in a bad shape,' said Catherine. 'When would you like to meet me?'

'Tomorrow is Saturday. I wonder if you could spare some time.'

'Listen, my husband and I are going out for lunch. But I could meet you for a coffee around ten in the morning.'

We decided to meet outside Lido on Champs Elysees at ten.

I had been waiting for some time when Catherine walked up to me a little out of breath.

'I am so sorry for being late. This awful traffic!'

'Don't worry, I have been here only for a few minutes,' I said.

We walked into the nearest café.

'What will you have?' I asked.

'An espresso will do. I am in a hurry. Thierry, my husband, dropped me here and has gone to see a friend in a hotel nearby. He should be back in half an hour. We are visiting my aunt near Versailles for lunch.'

I ordered a hot chocolate.

'I am so grateful you could spare some time. You can imagine how desperate I am to talk to someone about Emilie. She seems to be at the end of the road.'

'Frankly, the doctors have almost given up. The last chemotherapy, they said, was a final effort. She has been suffering for almost three years now. She seemed to have come out of it at one stage, but it has come back with a vengeance and I shudder to think of losing such a precious friend.'

'Must be harsh on her family,' I said.

'She has no family. Her mother passed away long ago. She has an uncle in Poitiers who visits her once in a while. And then there are her friends. Her employers have been very nice. The head of the biotech company she has been working for in Paris, Mr Didier Pascal has been very helpful. He keeps a regular tab on her.'

'Didn't she marry?'

'No. She was miserable having left you. But she was in an awful situation then. She was finding it difficult to cope with her work and look after her crippled mother. So she shifted to Poitiers and took up a lighter job there. She also got some help from her uncle's family. Years later, after her mother had passed away and she could think of her own life, she often said she had been unfair to you and was sure you had taken her decision very badly.'

'She told me so and said she didn't get in touch with me because she thought I might have moved on in my life. She was wrong then too. I wish she had not taken all those one-sided decisions.'

'You can't blame her. She has not had an easy life.'

'I realise what she has been through. But why didn't she get married?'

'She was afraid of building up another relationship. She did come across some men but it never went beyond friendship.'

'I wish we could do something to help her.'

'You just have to pray and hope for the best.'

'I guess that's the best one can do for the moment, but I wish we could do something more. I find it revolting to just sit around while Emilie is fighting for her life.'

Catherine sighed, 'You don't know how frustrated I have felt all this while.'

'I can imagine.'

'Listen, I must go now. Thierry must be waiting in the next by-lane in our car.'

'Let me accompany you to your car,' I said.

Catherine introduced me to Thierry. He seemed a pleasant person.

'Catherine told me about you. It's good you are here. Emilie needs all the care she can get at this stage,' he said.

'But it seems there is very little all of us can do for her.'

'That's unfortunately the case. But let's hope she will pull through. Don't hesitate to contact us for any help. In any case, Catherine visits Emilie as often as she can.'

I thanked Thierry and they departed, leaving me alone once again to my anguish.

Emilie was asleep when I stepped into her room. I quietly took the chair by her bedside. It was sometime before she opened her eyes.

'How are you feeling?'

'Not too good, I am afraid. I feel too weak.'

'Don't worry. Maybe it's because of chemotherapy.'

'They did some scans today to see if the last round of chemotherapy has been beneficial. The results should be available tomorrow.'

'I am sure they will have positive findings.'

'Let's hope so.'

The plump nurse walked in.

'Time to take your temperature and blood pressure, Mademoiselle Martin,' she announced and proceeded to take the measurements. When she was finished, Emilie asked her if they had received the scan results.

'Not yet,' said the plump nurse. 'We should have them tomorrow. In any case I am not authorized to comment on those results. Dr Beaujean will examine them and talk to you tomorrow.'

'Around what time would that be? I would like to be present when the doctor is ready to talk of the results,' I said.

'I'll speak to the doctor on phone and let you know in a little while.' The nurse left.

'Have you been moving around a bit in Paris?' Emilie asked.

'Not much. I went to Notre Dame the other day and prayed for your recovery. It gave me peace of mind.'

'How could I ever thank you for all the care you have been bestowing on me for the last few days despite my having caused so much suffering to you?'

'You don't have to be so formal,' I protested.

'In a few days, the new year will come. I wish we could usher it in together at Charles de Gaulle etoile as we did once,' said Emilie with a smile.

'Well we will do so next year.'

'It would be so nice if we could do all those things together again. All the dancing, eating, seeing movies, visiting museums, reading.'

'It's amazing how we have been thinking of the same things. I can't wait to see you recovered from your illness and do all those lovely things together.'

Emilie smiled.

The plump nurse came in.

'Dr Beaujean will be here around this time tomorrow. So if you come as usual during visitors' hour, you should be able to see him,' she told me.

'Remember, you are not alone in all this. We are all with you. All your friends are praying for you. I am sure everything will turn out well,' I told Emilie as I left her.

'I know that,' she said.

I was on tenterhooks the next twenty-four hours. What must Emilie be going through, I often asked myself. 'Please give Emilie a long life, O' God. Give us back our old days of happiness,' I prayed.

Finally I was in the hospital waiting for the doctor's verdict on the life of a woman who was so dear to me.

Dr Beaujean arrived and greeted Emilie with a smile. He took a chair next to her bed. Emile and I were waiting for his word with bated breath.

'How have you been, Mademoiselle?' he asked.

'I feel too weak and find it more and more difficult to eat, even in small quantities.'

'Mademoiselle, you have been so courageous all through this disease. I have often admired your brave nature and ability to bear pain. I have always spoken to you openly and frankly and shall do so today.'

My heart ducked a beat. What was he arriving at?

Dr Beaujean fell silent momentarily and looked down as if not wanting to say what he was going to say. He then looked Emilie squarely in the eye and continued, 'I am afraid I don't have good news for you. The scan results show that chemotherapy has not been effective. Your disease is spreading fast and we seem to have no more options.'

Emilie stared silently at the doctor's face for a few seconds and then said, 'Thank you for being forthright as always. You said there seem to be no more options.'

'That's what I said. I shall consult some colleagues over the next day or so to see if anything further can be done, although I have little hope of coming up with something that could help you.'

'How much more time do I have?'

'One can never be certain about these things.'

'How much more time do I have? You must be honest with me.'

'Life and death are not things human beings can comment on with any degree of certainty. But from my past experience, I would say two to three weeks, perhaps a little more or a little less.'

Emilie extended her hand to me. I held it gently.

'I am sorry I have not been able to help you this time around. However, I would like to assure you that we shall keep you as comfortable as possible. Try to eat as much as you can, in small quantities. We have been giving you a mild tranquilliser. You must take maximum possible rest. If you need, the nurse will give you an injection to enable you have good sleep.'

I had sat through the whole conversation in a daze. It seemed as if it was a bad dream.

Finally, the import of the doctor's words dawned on me. 'Could I see you tomorrow after you have consulted some of your colleagues?' I asked.

'Sure. I shall be available here around the same time in the evening. Mademoiselle Martin, I must go now, but I shall come anytime you need me. Remember I shall still try to do whatever I can for you. Au revoir.'

'Au revoir,' both Emilie and I said.

The doctor left.

'Well, that's it. I seem to have lost the battle for my life,' said Emilie.

'Precisely because it is the battle for your life, you should not give up so easily,' I said cupping her face in my hands.

'The doctor said there are no more options.'

'But he also said he was going to consult some other doctors. I too shall speak to some people in the medical research community. I am sure something can be done even at this stage. You yourself have been involved in medical research. You know that researchers don't give up so easily.'

'No they don't, but it's also a frustrating experience when you can't come up with cures for diseases even as they continue to kill thousands around the world.'

'Remember that you are not alone in this. You have the good wishes of all your friends. I am with you and I am not going to give up and will not let you do that.'

'Can you request Catherine to come tomorrow? I need to tie up the disposal of my personal belongings and some money I have in bank and investment accounts.'

'I shall certainly ask her to come tomorrow, but I insist that we are not going to give up. Our fight must continue till there is the slightest chance of getting some help for you.'

'I feel very tired and weak. I could not sleep well last night. Maybe I should take a tranquilliser injection. Could you please talk to the nurse?'

I had myself not been able to sleep well the previous night and I could imagine the level of Emilie's angst.

'Ok, I'll be back in a minute.'

I went to the nurses' station. The plump nurse was around.

'Emilie wants to take a tranquilliser injection.'

'It will be better if she takes it a little later in the evening so that she could sleep peacefully through the night. I shall be with you in a minute and talk to her.'

'She seems understandably anxious,' I said.

'She has been such a brave woman, but I realise what she must be going through.'

'Dr Beaujean says nothing further can be done.'

'He knows what he is saying. He is one of our best doctors in the field.'

'The visitors' hour is coming to an end and I don't want to leave Emilie alone. She needs company to pull through the terrible frame of mind the doctor's verdict has put her in.'

'Don't worry. We are here to see to it that she is not left alone to her anxiety. In a little while, Mme Bridier from Cooperation Contre Cancer will be here to spend some time with her.'

The nurse came with me to Emilie and said it would be better if the injection was taken later in the evening. She also told her about Mme Bridier and left.

'Mme Bridier is such a fine person.' Emilie told me, ' She is a volunteer belonging to an NGO and has visited me on a few occasions in the past. She herself has been a cancer patient, but has managed to stay on top of it so far. She is so nice to talk to.'

Within a few minutes Mme Bridier walked in. She was a middle-aged lady with a warm face.

'Meet Mme Bridier,' Emilie introduced her, 'and this is Lalit my friend.'

'Very pleased to meet you,' Mme Bridier extended her hand.

'I am sorry I haven't been able to come for the last few days, but Dr Beaujean told me you may need some help. So here I am and I shall visit you as often as you want,' said Mme Bridier.

'Thank you. It's so reassuring to have you around,' said Emilie.

With the visitors' hour coming to a close, I had to leave. I told Emilie I would be back the next day and in the meanwhile would explore what further could be done

I called Catherine later that evening and told her about Emilie.

'Oh God! It's dreadful,' Catherine's voice was quivering with emotion.

'She wants you to visit her tomorrow. She wishes to tie up disposal of her personal belongings and money.'

'Please don't say all this. I can't bear it any more. Please Lalit, say she is going to get well,' Catherine was on the verge of crying.

'Could you visit her tomorrow? I am sure she will find emotional comfort in you. I too can't bear the thought of her leaving us. The doctor says no more options are left. I refuse to give up so easily.'

'I shall certainly visit her tomorrow.'

'Catherine, she is at the end of the road. We need to speak to some medical researchers to see if she can be helped in any way even at this stage. New treatments keep appearing on the horizon every day.'

'The best person to speak to would be Didier Pascal, Emilie's boss. He is bound to know some researchers on cancer. I think I have his phone number. I spoke to him on behalf of Emilie on one or two occasions. I shall try to speak to him today and let you know if he can suggest something,' said Catherine.

'I don't know how to thank you for being so helpful.'

'Lalit, I have known Emilie ever since we were together in school. How I wish some miracle would save her.'

'Let's hope a miracle would come about. I shall be in touch with you,' I said.

I called Claude and requested him also to speak to some of his friends about Emilie. He expressed his sympathies and promised to see if he could come up with something. Not feeling hungry, I came back to my hotel room, opened a bottle of wine and sat in front of the TV. In the next hour or so, I downed several glasses of wine. My gaze was fixed on the TV screen, but my mind was elsewhere. All that I registered were snatches of prime time news followed by bits and pieces of a movie. As the wine took effect, my spirits rose a little. God will be kind to us, I thought. He wouldn't have brought us together after such a long time only to take Emie away from me. Hope turned into despair again when the effect of wine started to wane. I was exhausted and slumped in my chair. The phone rang. It was Catherine.

'I could speak to Didier. He mentioned one Dr Roche working in a medical research establishment in Toulouse. Apparently, he is known for some pioneering research in cancer treatment. Didier said he would speak to him tomorrow and let me know what he has to say. He has also promised to contact some other friends of his in the medical fraternity.'

'Thanks so much, Catherine. I shall see you at the hospital tomorrow during visitors' hour. Do get in touch if you hear anything from Didier before that.'

'I shall do that. But let me also give you his phone numbers. You could contact him sometime during the day.'

I noted the numbers hoping that they would open up some avenue the next day.

I called Didier Pascal from the Remedes factory around noon the next day.

'Monsieur Pascal, my name is Lalit Khanna. I am a friend of Emilie Martin. Catherine Leblanc spoke to you yesterday.'

'Ah yes, she gave me this terrible news. I visited Emilie some two weeks ago and things didn't look good. It's such a blow for all of us – her friends and well wishers.'

'Monsieur Pascal, I wonder if you were able to speak to someone in the cancer research circles.'

'I did manage to speak to this friend of mine in Toulouse, Dr Roche. He has been in cancer research for years now. He has for the last few years been working on angiogenesis inhibitors for cancer treatment. You see, a malignant tumour needs to acquire a network of blood vessels to get nutrients and oxygen. Angiogenesis inhibitors seek to deny this blood vessels network to the cancer to prevent its growth and spread. Roche has recently got permission for clinical trial of one such medicine.'

'Does he think it could help Emilie?' I asked eagerly.

'The stage at which she is, he has doubts if he can help. But he is coming here in three days on 23 December to spend Christmas with his family. He says he could look at Emilie's medical record and meet Dr Beaujean, if possible, to see if he can be of any help.'

'That would indeed be very kind of him. I shall speak of this to Dr Beaujean later today to see if he can meet Dr Roche on the 23rd.'

'Good then, let's remain in touch and in the meanwhile I am also trying to contact some other researchers here in Europe and in the United States.'

'Thank you so much Monsieur Pascal.'

My condition was that of a person, thrown into choppy seas by a shipwreck, who struggles to find the smallest plank to hold on to. The Roche medicine looked like one such plank in that state of desperation.

I called Claude later in the afternoon. He said he had spoken to two doctors. As it happened, Dr Beaujean had also spoken to one of them earlier in the day. Both of them said that given Emilie's condition, nothing could be done. Both also told Claude that Dr Beaujean was a highly competent doctor and we could be sure that if anything could be done, he would do it.

It was visitors' hour. Catherine and I were with Emilie. She didn't look good at all. She said she had been able to sleep the previous night after she was given an injection. But she had felt restless throughout the day and had experienced breathing problem. They had given her some medicines to help.

'Listen, I want you to do something for me,' Emilie turned to Catherine.

'I'll be happy to help in any way I can,' said Catherine.

'I am left with a week or two and I want you to dispose off my personal possessions and money.'

Catherine kept quiet, trying to fight tears.

'You'll have to speak to my landlord to terminate the lease of my apartment. Explain to him the circumstances and pay him whatever rent needs to be paid. I shall issue a transfer order from my account. I think you have his phone number. You spoke to him once earlier.'

Catherine, who was looking down to hide her face, nodded.

'Amongst my personal belongings, there is a box containing some items of my parents – their wedding album, some special gifts they had given each other. These should remain in the family. Please pass that box on to my uncle. I sent him a message yesterday and he is coming to see my in a day or so. The box could be given to him then.'

Catherine was desperately trying to hide her eyes that were brimming with tears.

'Then there is a box in the lower drawer of my bedside table which contains the letters Lali wrote to me and our photographs. Please give it to Lali. Gift my collection of books to the municipal library near my house. Sell all other belongings and donate the money, along with the funds in my bank accounts, to Medecins Sans Frontieres. They bring succour to so many helpless people in the world.'

'For God's sake, stop it Emilie,' Catherine finally burst out, 'you are not going anywhere.' Tears were rolling down her cheeks. Emilie was also sobbing. I felt as if someone was tearing my insides apart, but maintained my composure in order not to upset Emilie any further.

When Emile regained control of herself, she said, 'Look, even talking is somewhat of a strain for me now. But I have spoken so much with an effort because what I have told you is important to me. Please get a lawyer to prepare a legal paper authorising you to dispose of my belongings and money. Details of my bank accounts are in a file in my bedroom cupboard. You already have all the keys.'

'Of course, I shall do whatever you want me to do,' said Catherine with a faint smile, wiping her tears, 'but let me tell you that you are not going anywhere. We will all fight alongside you to defeat your disease.'

'Thank you,' said Emilie with an expression of relief on her face and fell silent, looking listless, her eyes shut.

My gaze briefly caught sight of Catherine's eyes. She was again on the brink of tears. I gestured to her not to cry. She put a handkerchief on her eyes, but her heavy breathing revealed the turmoil inside her.

Dr Beaujean walked in.

'How are you, Mademoiselle?' he asked his familiar question.

Emilie slowly opened her eyes.

'Not too good, I am afraid,' she said.

'Well, we are starting some new medicines to keep you at ease. We will give you oxygen at regular intervals. You could again take a tranquilliser injection today if you have difficulty sleeping.'

Dr Beaujean fell silent for a few seconds. We were all looking eagerly at his face to see if he would say anything further. He said nothing and finally when he spoke, all that he said was that he would come again the next day and could be approached by the nurses on phone if any help was required in the meanwhile.

As he left the room, I caught up with him.

'Doctor, can I speak to you for a minute?'

'O, sure,' he said, guiding me towards a corner of the hospital corridor.

'Were you able to speak to some of your colleagues to see if anything can be done?'

'Yes, I have spoken to some and they all think nothing further can be done. I believe we need to accept the reality. It's a matter of days or weeks.'

'I have been in touch with a friend, who has spoken to one Dr Roche in Toulouse. They have a trial drug that inhibits angiogenesis.'

'I know about that drug and Dr Roche's research. But I don't think it can help Mademoiselle Martin. Besides, the medicine has painful side effects and will not be worth it.'

'Dr Roche is coming here on the 23rd and has agreed to assess Emilie's case. I wonder if he could meet you and also look at Emilie's medical record. I am fully conscious of Emilie's condition, but we just wish to explore every available avenue, if only to give her a little more time. I hope you understand.'

'I realise your dilemma. I shall be happy to meet Dr Roche.'

Dr Beaujean consulted his electronic diary and said he would be in hospital between three and four in the afternoon on the 23rd and would be happy to meet Dr Roche in case he came during that time. The nurses would have his instructions to show Emilie's record to Dr Roche in case he came at any other time.

I came back to Emilie's room. Her eyes were shut and she had laboured breathing.

Catherine and I sat silently until she opened her eyes.

'I spoke to Dr Beaujean, said I. 'He has agreed to meet a doctor, Pascal has been in touch with in Toulouse, who has a new trial drug for cancer. We are trying to organise the meeting in two days' time on the 23rd. I am hopeful we may come across a way out that day.'

Emilie nodded.

'See I told you that we will not give up. God willing something will work out,' said Catherine to cheer Emilie up.

'Thank you,' said Emilie in an exhausted voice.

Mrs Bridier had arrived by the time we left. Some dedication, I thought.

I came back to my hotel, called Dr Pascal and told him about Dr Beaujean's willingness to meet Dr Roche. Pascal said he would try to organise Roche's visit between three and four. I then called Udai in India. It was late in the evening. He and Shobha had just come back from a dinner. I told him about my having met Emilie and her illness.

'It's terrible. We will pray to God to help her.'

I asked Udai to check with Shobha if she had the ring that I had given her years ago to keep in her jewellry collection. Udai spoke to Shobha and said she vaguely recollected the ring and that it should be in her jewellry box kept in a bank locker.

'Can you rush it to me in the next two days?' I asked.

'Look, Shobha has to locate it first and I'll check with my friend in the Air France office here if one of their crew can carry it for you.'

'This is important,' I said.

'I realise it. And please stay in Paris for as long as necessary to see Emilie through her illness,' said Udai.

'Thanks. But I don't have the heart to see her through to her end.'

'You must remain courageous to give her strength. Remember, we will all pray for her.'

'Thanks, Udai and don't forget the ring.'

I had been waiting in the hospital for over half an hour when Pascal, accompanied by Roche, walked in. They went straight into a meeting with Dr Beaujean. I was asked to wait outside. The meeting would have lasted for no more than twenty minutes, but it seemed as if they had made me wait a lifetime for their decision. I had my eyes shut throughout, with a prayer for Emilie on my lips. Other enquiries of Pascal and Claude had not turned up anything. The deliberations going on in Dr Beaujean's office were the last medical hope for Emilie. Will they come out and sustain it or dash it saying they wished to be frank and did not want to give any false hope? 'O God, let them come out and say they can still do something for Emie! Please do not take away our last ray of hope!' Emilie's life seemed to hang by a slender thread – Roche's medicine. If it broke, she would go crashing into the dark abyss of death underneath, never to emerge from it again. Finally, Dr Beaujean stepped out to call me inside. I went in with a throbbing heart and took a chair. Within seconds, the feared words of Dr Beaujean were hitting my eardrums like a thunderbolt: 'We have discussed Emilie's case thoroughly. We don't believe Dr Roche's angiogenesis inhibitor will do her any good.'

'Can't you try it, just in case it gives her a little more time?' I pleaded.

'Medical ethics do not permit us to try the drug on a patient who has no chance whatsoever of benefiting from it.' This time it was Dr Roche who spoke. 'Besides, this medicine has serious side effects such as severe joint and muscle pains, which get reversed once the treatment is stopped. But Mademoiselle Martin does not even have the time for the medicine to show any impact. It would be unwise to put her through so much of pain to try a remedy that we are sure is of no use. Our effort now should be to see her through her ordeal in as painless a manner as possible. I am awfully sorry; we are not of any help.'

For a few seconds, I sat bewildered, moving my gaze from one face to the other, hoping that one of them would come out with some other hope to cling on to. 'See her through her ordeal' were polite words. But see her through to what? Death.

The central issue was not her current suffering but what was staring her in the face at the end of this suffering. For the doctors, she was just another patient, whose time had run out and who should now be seen through to as painless an end as possible. Emotions were not their problem and rightly so. They had done their best for Emilie. They were used to seeing this happen to other patients and were required by their profession to remain emotionally detached from such situations. It was not the same for me. I could not bear the thought of Emilie being seen through to her death, even if painlessly. And what about Emilie herself? What must be going through her mind?

I was shaken out of my thoughts by Dr Beaujean, 'Look, we are duty bound to be honest with you and above all with our patients. I told you earlier and I repeat it. It's a matter of days or weeks now. The sooner we accept this reality, the better for all of us. We have just made a last attempt to see if anything can still be done for her and the answer is no.' 'I thank you for all that you have done,' is all that I managed to say. I got up, shook hands with the doctors. Pascal said he would come with me to see Emilie for a few minutes.

A man was sitting by Emilie's bedside. Emilie introduced us to him. It was her uncle from Poitiers.

'Emilie told me how much you have done for her. I don't know how to thank you. It's good to know you are here. I must go now, but I shall visit Emilie again in two-three days,' Emilie's uncle said as he shook hands with me.

He kissed Emilie on her forehead and said, 'You have always been such a bold girl. I have seen you stand by your mother like a rock through thick and thin. Keep up your spirits. I shall be back soon.'

Everyone was advising Emilie to stay brave knowing full well that she was in a situation that would shatter even the most courageous. 'What must be going through her mind?' was the question tormenting me.

'How are you Emilie?' Pascal asked.

'Trying to stay afloat.'

'Everyone at work misses you.'

'I too miss them. I wish I could be with all of you.'

'Well, your contribution to the research is very much with us.'

'How is the research going?'

'O, we are making slow progress, but you know a researcher is never happy with the pace of advancement. We always want things to go much faster, especially when it comes to medical research to alleviate human suffering.' Emilie nodded in agreement.

Pascal left saying he would be in touch and could be contacted if he could be of any help.

I sat by Emilie's side, my eyes transfixed on the floor. I was desperately trying to avoid her gaze. Finally, she spoke up.

'Uncle went to my apartment with Catherine and has taken away the box of my parents' belongings. It's such a relief.'

'That's good.'

'Did the doctor from Toulouse come?'

'He was here.'

'What did he say?'

'He talked to DrBeaujean. Pascal was also present. They believe his medicine cannot be of much use to you.'

There was no reaction on Emilie's face. She had got too used to such statements of total despair. She closed her eyes and I kept mine transfixed on the floor – looking at nothing in particular. My mind was again digging through the memories of the good days we had spent together.

'Uncle spoke of the Lourdes shrine,' Emilie's voice shook me out of my thoughts.

'What did you say?'

'My uncle spoke of the Lourdes shrine and said he would get me water from the Lourdes spring when he visits me next. He has some lying at home. It's believed to have healing power.'

'That's so nice of him.'

'I had gone to Lourdes with my parents and brother in my childhood. It's such a fine place. I wish I could go there and pray at the shrine.'

'I too have heard of the famous healing water from the Lourdes shrine.'

The nurse came and put Emilie on oxygen.

'What was going through Emilie's mind?' The question besieged me again. Was her fortitude cracking? What else could one expect? My head was throbbing with countless thoughts crisscrossing it. Mrs Bridier arrived and it was time for me to leave.

I called Catherine from my hotel.

'How is she?' Catherine asked.

'She seems to be sinking fast.' There was silence at the other end.

'Listen, Emilie's uncle spoke to her about the Lourdes water which is believed to have healing qualities.'

'Yes, it's a famous shrine.'

'I have heard of it. Where exactly is it located?'

'It's close to the French-Spanish border.'

'Emilie's uncle said he has some Lourdes water lying at his home and would bring it when he visits Emilie the next time. I wonder if I could visit Lourdes in the next two-three days, pray there for Emilie and bring the water for her.'

'Why don't you talk to Thierry? He should be able to guide you on how to go there.' Catherine passed on the phone to Thierry. He said the easiest way might be to fly down to

Toulouse and then drive down to Lourdes – a drive of about two hours. He offered to help me to get air bookings – not an easy task in the holiday season that we were in – and to tie up car hiring at the Toulouse airport. I asked him to get me the air bookings to go to Toulouse on the morning of the 26th of December and to come back the same evening. I told him that car hiring might not be necessary as I had a friend in Toulouse who might agree to drive me down to Lourdes. I again spoke to Catherine and we decided to visit Emilie together the next day, which would be the Christmas Eve.

I called Sunil Wickramsinghe in Toulouse. He said he would gladly drive me down to Lourdes. He had been keeping track of Emilie's condition and said that he and Brigitte were planning to visit her in the coming days.

The next day, Catherine and I went to the hospital together. The plump nurse was at the nurses' station. She said Emilie had been very bad the whole day. She was having increasing breathing problem as the capacity of her lungs was diminishing fast.

Christmas decorations had been put up in Emilie's room by the hospital staff. Catherine had carried along a small Christmas tree that she put in one corner of the room.

Emilie was on oxygen. She acknowledged our arrival by momentarily opening her eyes. She was clearly in a great deal of discomfort and breathing with difficulty. We sat quietly by her side.

Emilie woke up briefly.

'I am visiting Lourdes the day after to pray for you and to bring some water from the spring there.'

Her lips moved as if to say 'Thank you' and she shut her eyes again.

'Will you be going for the Christmas mass this evening?' I asked Catherine as we left the hospital.

'Yes, Thierry and I will go to our church.'

'May I accompany you?'

'Sure you may. We will pick you up from your hotel.'

'Thanks.'

This was the second time I was attending the midnight Christmas mass. I had once accompanied a Christian friend to a mass in India long ago.

The atmosphere in the church was serene and soothing. The musical notes and Christmas carols, floating past my ears, calmed my nerves to some extent. People were in a joyous mood and singing with great zest. I sat right through with my eyes shut, praying to God to do something for Emilie. 'Aren't you being foolish? Nothing can cure Emilie now.' The thought crossed my mind two-three times. I suppressed it. I persisted with my prayer, beseeching God to help Emilie. Prayer and Lourdes water now seemed to be the only barriers between Emilie and her end. How could I lose faith in these anchors?

The following day was bright and sunny but very cold. I met a nurse coming out of Emilie's room and asked how she was. She said Emilie's breathing was slightly better and she was off oxygen for some time. She hastened to add that this had nothing to do with her fundamental condition that was continuing to deteriorate. It was just one of those spells of transitory relief that can crop up even in the case of sinking patients.

'Merry Christmas, Emilie,' I said putting on as cheerful an expression as I could.

'Merry Christmas,' she whispered.

'Soon after your visit to India, I had bought a ring for you. Just a simple ring with my meager savings from the monthly allowance my father had started giving me. I had hoped to give it to you long back, but then we lost touch. Udai has rushed it to me through a friend in Air France and here it is.'

I took the ring out of my pocket. Emilie extended her finger and I slipped it on.

'Thank you, Lali. It's so pretty,' she said.

'I am sorry I have no gift for you. But let me give you something you were always chasing me for – a kiss.' I bent down and kissed her lips gently.

'That's the greatest gift you could have given me,' I said.

I turned my face away to hide the tears welling up in my eyes. I recalled how I used to pester her for a kiss ever so often twenty years ago. Once I had told her that I wished I could glue my lips permanently to hers.

'How will we go to work then?' she had asked and we had both burst out laughing.

'The city must be looking dazzling at this time,' Emilie said.

'It is, with all the Christmas decorations.'

'Christmas festivities followed by the New Year, all the colours in nature, each season bringing its own charms, the brightness of the day following every night. Life offers us all these and many more bounties. Caught in the rush of life, I never took note of them. Now that these are about to be denied to me forever, I can't bear the thought of losing them.'

I wiped two tears that had trickled down Emilie's temples. Her words, particularly 'forever', had fallen on me like lightning. I did not know what to say.

'I am going to Lourdes tomorrow to pray for you,' is all that I managed to utter.

Emilie's breathing was becoming laborious. I called the nurse who put her on oxygen.

'Shobha has sent something for you,' I told Emilie when her breathing stabilised a bit.

'She prayed for you at the temple our family visits regularly. The priest gave her some flowers as his blessings. He is known to have brought relief to many suffering people. Shobha has asked me to place these flowers by your bedside.'

I took out five marigold flowers, Shobha had sent along with the ring, and put them on Emilie's bedside table.

I took an early morning flight to Toulouse on the 26th. Sunil was at the airport and drove me to Lourdes. On the way we talked of the pleasant times we had spent together. Sunil tried to lift my spirits by saying that I had taken the right decision in coming to pray at Lourdes. A very large number of people visited the place every year and it was known to have alleviated the suffering of many.

As we were trying to get information at the Lourdes sanctuary, we saw an Asian priest. He smiled at us. I introduced myself. He said he was Father Jose Kurien, a Catholic priest from Kerala. He offered to take us around the sanctuary, but said he must first explain its history to us. In 1858, in the grotto of Massabielle near Lourdes, Virgin Mary appeared eighteen times to Bernadette Soubirous, a peasant girl of the area. She said that a chapel be built at the site where she had appeared and asked Bernadette to drink from a fountain in the grotto. Bernadette could find no fountain, but when she dug a spot pointed out by the apparition, a spring appeared. The water from this spring, said Father Kurien, is widely known to have healing power. It was after four years of investigations that official recognition was given to the apparitions in January 1862 and seven miraculous healings were noted. Bernadette, who died in 1879, was beatified in 1925 and canonised by Pope Pius XI in 1933. Kurien told us that more than five million people visited the Lourdes sanctuary every year from all parts of the world.

Later on, we passed through the grotto to see the spring. The place brought a sudden feeling of peace and calm on me.

All through, my mind was dominated by just one sentence: 'O God, please help Emilie!'

I had obtained a bottle of Lourdes water. Father Kurien invited us to have a quick meal at his house before leaving for Toulouse. He said he would give us typical Kerala food. It was an offer I could not resist. The last I had eaten delicious Kerala food was during my vacation there some six years ago. Father Kurien served us boiled rice with hot Rasam and a tapioca and fish curry he had cooked the previous evening. He said he normally had local dishes, but cooked Kerala food every now and then with ingredients he brought from Indian shops in Paris. He wished he could make it more often, but just didn't have the time needed for elaborate cooking.

Our talk focused on the Lourdes shrine. Kurien told us about each of the eighteen appearances of Virgin Mary.

'I am glad I came here. As you can imagine, the last few weeks have been a period of great anguish for me – seeing a dear friend moving towards her end. Coming here has given me peace of mind. I hope our prayers help Emilie,' I said.

'Our prayers will certainly help her. Have faith in God. He will surely lighten her suffering,' said Kurien. He was silent for a few seconds and then resumed,' We must remember that only God is immortal. Dust man is and to dust he will return. Life must decay and die. Even as a mighty tree rots and falls, saplings have already taken roots to take its place. Similarly, even as human beings pass on, others take birth to carry forward this beautiful stream of existence. If life did not perish, there will be no place for its renewal.'

'Thank you. Thank you very much for your kind help,' I mumbled.

The next day I visited Emilie. I asked the nurse if she could remove the oxygen mask. She said it could be done only for a few minutes.

Emilie opened her eyes. She was already on a drip and could hardly swallow anything. I dabbed a few drops of Lourdes water on her lips.

'I prayed at the Lourdes shrine yesterday. So many suffering people come there for relief and cure.'

'Thank you,' Emilie mumbled.

She opened her eyes after a few seconds and tried to say something. She was barely audible. I moved my ear close to her mouth.

'Do you remember the holy man who delivered a discourse at your house when I was in India?'

'Yes, I do.'

'He said soul never dies.'

'Yes he did and I believe he knew what he was saying.'

Emilie had become breathless. I called the nurse who put her back on oxygen.

Over the next six days, Emilie's condition worsened sharply. The number of leads from her body to monitors and tubes in her mouth and nose multiplied. Finally, the horrible moment arrived. I stood helplessly in one corner of the room as a doctor and a nurse watched over Emilie. The monitor beep of her heartbeat became increasingly erratic, got progressively spaced out and then went completely flat.

The doctor's dreaded words rang in my ears, 'I am sorry. She is no more.'

So the doctors had done the best they could under the circumstances. Emilie had been seen through – seen through to her death relatively painlessly. That is without much pain visible or perceptible to those of us left behind. Soon her last rites would be performed. Catherine had completed the necessary paper work and would over the next few days dispose of Emilie's worldly possessions. Lovely Emilie would then become just a memory in this world – a mere memory till those carrying her memory in their minds themselves became memories in this world. I broke down. The doctor put his hand on my shoulder and walked away.

Four days later, I was seated in an Air India plane waiting on the tarmac in a queue to take off from Charles de Gaulle airport for Delhi. I had decided to take a break and come back later to complete my work with Remedes. Udai had insisted that I came back to be with the family to get over my grief.

Exhaustion had overwhelmed my body and it cried out for rest. But the storm blowing in my mind had not permitted me even a wink of sleep. My eyes were bloodshot with lack of sleep. Why did it have to end this way? The question flashed through my mind time and again. Why had I found Emilie only to lose her again? I repeatedly recalled the joyful months I had spent with her during my first visit to France. The pleasant memories came streaming like the scenes of a film in front of my eyes. The joy that I had experienced when she had for the first time shown interest in me. The blissful time that we had spent in love with each other. The charm that Emilie's beauty had exercised on me. And above all her caring nature that I had come to admire so much. Then I had lost her when she decided to break off with me. I had agonised over her decision, but had eventually come to terms with it. She had the right to live her life the way she wanted, I had rationalised. Years later, she had unexpectedly come back in my life only to leave me again and this time forever. She was gone forever and not to live her life the way she wanted. Her life had been snatched away by a horrible disease. She was dead. Why did it have to happen this way? People would say it was destined to be so. But who had destined it to be so and why? I had no answers.

Emilie's last rites had been performed in the presence of a small group of family and friends. Before I left Paris, I had made it a point to meet Mrs Bridier to thank her for her care and dedication in Emilie's last days. We met at a café near Trocadero.

'Emilie was a brave woman, but there is a limit to bravery,' Mrs Bridier had said. She explained that her attempt had been to calm Emilie's anxiety. She had told her that death was inevitable for everyone and that sooner or later it would be the fate of everyone to face it. She had counselled Emilie to put herself in the hands of God and leave everything to Him. One day, about ten days before her death, Emilie had suddenly asked Mrs Bridier, 'There is so much I could not do in this life. Do you think I will have another life to complete all that I wanted to do?'

Emilie's unexpected question had left Mrs Bridier speechless for a few moments, but she had quickly recovered to say, 'You have been such a good woman. I am sure God would like you to continue your fine work. You are going into a sleep and will certainly awaken on the day of Christ's coming.'

Everyone said Emilie had died, but nobody knew what exactly that meant. My mind went back for the zillionth time to the question as I sat waiting for the plane to take off. Had Emilie's soul survived to take birth again? Would she be reincarnated or resurrected? Nobody could say for sure. I had a belief but no definite answer. Others might have other beliefs but no definite answer. But did the absence of a definite answer matter so long as the thought of a possible existence after death gave her some solace in her last days?

The plane had gone above the cloud cover. The clouds beneath looked like mounds of cotton bathed in sun. The aircraft cabin was full of bright sunshine. I recalled that unable to sleep on

New Year's Eve, I had walked down from my hotel to Arc de Triomphe. Many old memories had welled up inside me. I had seen the beautiful stream of life flow in full vigour even as someone, I loved so dearly, lay on her deathbed. I looked up to see the smiling face of the child, in the seat ahead of mine, peering at me. 'Keep seated, otherwise you will fall down,' his mother shouted. The child waved at me before he sat down. Suddenly the smiling faces of the children in the orphanage in Delhi appeared before my eyes. There was so much more I needed to do for them. Young life was beckoning me to nurse it so that the beautiful stream of existence could continue to flow. Lost in these thoughts, I dozed off.